THE DSA SEASON ONE, BOOK SIX

BROKEN LOYALTIES

Also by Lou Paduano

The Greystone Saga

Signs of Portents
Tales from Portents
The Medusa Coin
Pathways in the Dark
A Circle of Shadows

Greystone-in-Training

Hammer and Anvil

The DSA

Season One
The Clearing
Promethean
The Bridge
Spectral Advocate
Dark Impulses

THE DSA SEASON ONE, BOOK SIX

BROKEN LOYALTIES

Lou Paduano

Eleven Ten Publishing LLC

GRAND ISLAND, NEW YORK

Eleven Ten Publishing LLC
282 Fareway Lane
Grand Island, NY 14072

Publisher's note: This is a work of fiction. Names, characters, places, and incidents either are the product of the author's imagination or are used fictitiously. Any resemblance to actual events, locales, or persons, living or dead, is entirely coincidental.

Printed in the United States of America
Edited by JD Book Services.
Cover art design by MiblArt

First edition published 2020

Library of Congress Cataloguing in Publication Data
Paduano, Lou
Broken Loyalties / Lou Paduano

LCCN: 2020900761
ISBN-13: 978-1-944965-28-0 (paperback)
ISBN-13: 978-1-944965-27-3 (eBook)

For Bo and Uncle Dan,
who always bring laughter to the chaos.

CHAPTER ONE

Susan Metcalf stared, and the woman in the mirror stared back. She judged her every brush stroke, the way her hair lay in thick tufts to the right. She quietly criticized the crease in her collar. No matter how hard she tried it refused to flatten.

She tore through the final knots in her hair. Her face was un-recognizable. Thin lines ran from her eyes. Flakes of dry skin covered her cheeks and brow from the unrelenting winter. Sadness penetrated once-strong blue irises. It was not a fear of lost youth, a terror of age creeping up on her out of nowhere. She had accepted how time ran counter to her wishes no matter the steps taken.

Her lack of recognition came from the growing number of compromises and mistakes that filled her days. Each stole from her, each pulled at her core and ripped an essential piece from what little remained of the woman who started this journey so long ago. Promises had been made, and quests had been under-taken and left incomplete. But time was a bitch of a thing, and when she fought against the rapidly draining hourglass all she managed to do was watch the sand empty in a pool on the floor.

Leaving the mirror behind, Metcalf tucked the brush away. The bed remained untouched, and the curtains were drawn as always. Little light followed her through the upstairs of the home. *Her* home. It was funny to call the residence that, though. Metcalf's name might have been on the tax statements and pub-lic records regarding the property, but it had never been her home. She had furnished it, made sure the kitchen remained stocked in coffee and other bare essentials—actually, pretty much only coffee. Beyond that it remained empty and devoid of life.

The domicile served to merely paint a picture for the casual observer. It was a place of residence to track her, to monitor her, though she rarely occupied the home. She paid a cleaning service to maintain the property. She never spoke to the neighbors and couldn't recall their names, though they were fully displayed on their mailboxes lining the road. Community was not her strong suit, and her weakness grew more apparent with each passing day.

It was a nice place, and it would have made a wonderful home for a family—all she needed was a pair of kids for the spare rooms on the second floor, maybe an entertainment center in the basement. The backyard stretched to the woods for plenty of exploring. She viewed the path as an escape route instead. Every aspect of her life was filtered through the lens of the mission she had served for decades. Now, she had to watch it crumble.

Because of her weaknesses.

Days had passed since she'd last stepped foot in the DSA warehouse, since she asked her personal assistant for a day to set things right and plan for what came next. She had never imagined the lull, never dreamed of the pause in the game played out by her enemies. Was she overly cautious or simply predicting the wrong outcome? Was this what Sullivan had warned her about: her inability to trust and reach out when needed? Had he been trying to help her instead of sabotage her at every turn?

The doorbell provided her answer. Her lip curled in a smirk. She had grown tired of the waiting and, at last, it was finished.

Metcalf took the stairs slowly, her steps defiant to the pressing of the bell in steady repetition. Each board creaked, announcing her arrival long before she reached the bottom. Her eyes sharpened with each footfall. Her posture straightened. This was no time for weakness. If this was to be the end, she would meet it straight on: strong and unyielding.

Two men waited on her stoop. She recognized them immediately. One was casual in his stance to hide his stature. The other met her gaze directly. He clutched a hand tight to his open badge while the other hovered close to his holster.

"Director Metcalf," Martin announced. The left side of his face was discolored from his recent altercation with Agent Riley.

The NSA logo gleamed in the sunlight. He took a step away, allowing her to open the outer glass door.

"Yes?" she asked, innocence in her voice. "Can I help you?"

Kanigher, Martin's long-time partner, shuffled closer. He held the door open for her and smiled. "We need you to come with us, Susan."

She leaned along the frame of the door. "What is this about?"

"Step over to the car, ma'am," Martin continued, unwilling to entertain questions. They followed orders, the only thing they truly understood.

Behind the pair on the stoop, another two agents took up positions along the sidewalk. A cargo van was parked in front of her property with a fifth man behind the wheel. All wore matching deep blue uniforms with the same insignia dotting the upper right. Despite the varied agencies they served, all now appeared to belong to a single entity.

The DSA.

Sullivan's move. It was time. Metcalf scanned the block. No neighbors poked their heads out. No innocents dotted the area.

"If I refuse?"

A pair of cuffs dangled between Kanigher's waiting fingers. Martin unclasped his holster and pulled out his Glock.

"You won't, Susan," Kanigher explained.

Behind the frame of the door, her fingers typed on her cell phone. When she finished, the message received with nothing but a smiley face in return, Metcalf dropped the device into her jacket pocket. She pulled the coat free from the hanger. She closed the door behind her and joined the agents.

"Let's go, then."

CHAPTER TWO
Five Days Earlier

She took her time walking to the car. The roads were covered by the flurry of snow bustling through the region. Large flakes continued to dance across the sky. They accompanied her through the dimly lit streets. The snow was serene, a peaceful distraction from multiple events vying for dominance in her exhausted thoughts.

She parked three blocks from the small home on Buffalo's West Side. Her boots crunched lightly from the sidewalk to the street. She was careful to allow oncoming traffic to depart before continuing her trek. Each delay held a second purpose, one achieved when a patter of steps began to trail her own. She reached for the handle to her car while trying to conceal the satisfaction on her face.

"Metcalf!" he called after her, and she finally dropped the pretense. When she had left him with as many open questions as she had, there was little doubt their conversation was not at an end. She counted on it, knowing his gift for insight and his inability to let things drop without some clarity.

Ben Riley demanded answers to *everything*. It was his greatest gift and his worst flaw. The call, the loud cry against the emptiness of the street, and the calm wind surrounding them stopped him at the corner. He scanned the area for signs of life. She did the same, both expecting enemies to jump out of the shadows.

They lived on borrowed time, the clock winding painfully down. His cheeks were flushed from the bitter temperatures, but his eyes pierced the darkness. She had made the right call with him, his strength, his will, and his unending perseverance.

"What is it, Ben?" she asked. She returned to the sidewalk from her waiting car.

He rubbed at his neck. He appeared emotionally drained from their conversation in the confines of his former partner's home. Emily Wright had gone missing soon after his recruitment. He blamed himself, though it lay squarely on Metcalf, the same as everything of late. She had tried to reassure him, to promise him some insight about Emily's whereabouts, but it did little to help.

"I haven't told Sullivan anything," he said. "I wouldn't."

"I appreciate that," she replied. She did, though the sentiment was lost in the telling. Her voice was always colder than intended; connecting with him or anyone was a constant struggle unless it centered on a lie. The truth of the matter was she wasn't certain *where* Ben fell in terms of loyalty. "Thank—"

"Don't thank me," Ben said with the shake of his head. "You may be a better liar than him, but you're both liars."

"I know." She had earned that ire. She had held back the truth for too long, stringing him along with missions and hope, but little in the way of a connection to the DSA. If she had offered more, told him about her link to his father, the whole situation might never have escalated. But she hadn't. She wasn't able to trust in herself to act like a friend because of her need to lead and control.

Yet she tried to make amends. She had left the DSA, her office, and her mission, to bring Ben back into the fold. She needed to win him over. It was a first step, and a necessary one for the fight ahead. She needed him when it all went to hell. Did he need her, though?

"This doesn't work if the lies continue."

"I know," she repeated.

"You have to tell me *everything*," he pressed. "Especially that bombshell about my old man. Open book or I walk."

"I understand."

"Do you?"

She held her tongue. Rushing any answer with Ben always rang false. He always took her quick reply as an outright lie. They both did. It was how they had operated since his arrival in Bethesda. She had played that game longer with the others at work.

When she had started as Director of the Department of Special Assignments, Metcalf was naive about the way of things. Hell, she was *still* learning how little she actually understood about the world surrounding the DSA. She came from a unique position and wanted that to be part of her strategy to make her department the best in its field. She wanted to make a difference. She also wanted to be honest with those around her and foster a team of like-minded and driven individuals capable of that great change. Instead, she had turned to a different path. She had recruited not the best in the business, but the fallen soldiers—the broken and disenfranchised.

The controllable.

"I do, Ben," she said in a whisper. Her eyes fell to the snow coating the ground, unblemished and pristine. "More than you know."

The young man with the bloodstained tie hesitated. He paced the corner. His gaze was torn between her and their surroundings. He was wary—much more so than when she offered him a spot on her team. Time at the DSA had changed him, and it hadn't been for the better. Now he worried about shadows, about the threats unseen: those she put in his path and those she hid from him.

He wasn't wrong. It had to stop. *She* had to stop.

"What happens next?"

Metcalf nodded, grateful he remained at her side. "Sullivan will make the opening move. Then things will happen fast. We have to be ready."

"I will be."

"I'm hoping it won't come to that," she continued. "I'm hoping that whatever aspirations the bastard has for the DSA will center on me, but seeing his actions here with Horace Waters and the lengths he's willing to go to hide his intentions, I'm not sure what to expect."

"You said he's looking for something?"

"The Wellspring."

"Where is it?" Ben asked. Her wayward glance gave her away. "You know, don't you?"

"No."

"Dammit, Metcalf, we just—"

"I'm not lying, Ben," she said. "I found the Wellspring, but it's in the wind right now thanks to my people. Intentionally."

"But Sullivan doesn't know that."

She sighed and turned skyward. Stars dotted the midnight sky, filtering between the thick, patchy clouds finishing their nightly deposit. The work was so clear when it was just her, when the thoughts centered on one action and one arena. What came next was bigger than that, larger than anything she had experienced during her career.

She feared the outcome. She also feared what she required from the man at her side. "I'm going to need you to do something for me, Ben. The way Sullivan's circled you since your recruitment? He thinks you know where the Wellspring is."

"I don't though." Frustration filled his words.

"He doesn't know that, and we can use that doubt," she said. "*You* can use it to help us buy time."

"How?"

She smiled. "I need you to make a call."

"I don't—"

Her hand fell on his shoulder. "This is where I ask you to trust me, Ben. For the sake of the DSA, and for everything we've been fighting for, I need your trust here and now or this all falls apart. Any answers you're looking for have to wait until this is over. I'll tell you everything once we're safe, but only you can make that possible."

The words sat with him for a long moment. With his sneakers settled deep into the billowing snow, he nodded. "I'll make your call, Metcalf. I'll play the bait."

"Thank—"

"I'm not done yet," he interrupted. "I need you to do something for me as well. A promise you damn well better keep."

"What?"

"This is where you show me how much I can trust you, Metcalf," Ben said under the Buffalo street lights. "Don't screw it up."

CHAPTER THREE

The cuffs remained in sight as Martin and Kanigher escorted Metcalf down the brick walkway to the waiting cargo van. The back door slid open to receive her. The agents at the sidewalk entered without a word.

Kanigher stopped at the end of the brick, his partner following suit. The latter kept his arm locked in Metcalf's to prevent her escape.

"What's up?" Martin asked.

Kanigher peered at the house. "You go ahead. I just want to check out the place, make sure she didn't leave any surprises."

Metcalf's eyes widened. "Robert, there's no reason—"

Martin sneered and kept her locked at his side. "I see what you mean. Good idea."

"I thought so," Kanigher said, passing along the set of cuffs.

"Dammit, Robert, you know me!" Metcalf yelled. She struggled against the tightening grip of Martin at her back.

Kanigher leaned close. "Exactly, Susan. That's why I don't trust you."

"This isn't right, Robert. You know this isn't—"

"Get out of here, Martin," Kanigher ordered, pointing to the van. "I'll meet you later."

"Sounds good." Martin pulled his captive to the sidewalk, then turned her toward the van. The door to the house opened and closed with a slam as it caught the wind. The sound caused her to jump, the finality of the exchange clear to her.

Her head slumped as they approached the van. Martin shoved her inside. A hand from one of the other agents caught her and helped her up the elevated step.

A lone bench positioned along the left-hand side offered seating for three. She took her place between the agents. Martin rounded the front of the van and headed for the passenger seat.

The right side of the van contained surveillance equipment for long-term stakeout operations. A large screen sat in the center, turned on yet not tuned in, causing static to fill the monitor. Martin reached for his ear on instinct, then settled along the seat before looking back at them.

"They're ready for her."

"Bully for them," Metcalf said with a grimace. She shifted uncomfortably, knocking auburn locks from her face.

Static faded from the screen. The NSA conference room took over the feed, a lone figure at its head. The portly soul folded his hands before him, a smug grin spread above Donald Stallworth's double chin.

"Susan."

"Donald," Metcalf replied through gritted teeth. Behind him, other members of the Inter-Agency Council stood in wait. The ruling body kept the DSA not only solvent but also a secret from their superiors.

Stallworth leaned back in his chair, grumbling under his breath. "The Council has been meeting all night to discuss matters at the DSA."

"You mean you were all at the same fundraiser, don't you?" Metcalf said. "I doubt you've put in a full day of work in years, Donald."

Stallworth sighed. "So you know what this is about. Excellent. That means we can skip the formalities."

"Please."

"You've forced this decision, Susan," Stallworth continued, tapping at the desk. "Ever since Agent Grissom's unfortunate loss, your command at the DSA has been questionable at best. There was the Bellbrook fiasco, the suspect nature of the Chicago operation, and what is this mess about Agent MacKenzie in Des Moines?"

"We're seeking him out. We're also still looking for the man behind the fiasco in Bellbrook as you so ineptly put it." Her anger forced the response, though the act satisfied none of the Council's desires. Their decision had already been made about her fate. They wouldn't have made the call if they hadn't. Her words were merely a final fight, she supposed.

"And failing," Stallworth said. "That's what this comes down to: a failure to lead. A failure to work with this Council. You're holding back, Susan, and it doesn't look good."

Her eyes thinned. "What are you saying, Donald?"

Stallworth stood, then leaned toward the screen. His jowls blocked the silent members of the Council. "You've been relieved of command, effective immediately. Additionally, the other members believe you know more of this Witness person's intents, so you've been remanded into custody."

"The Witness?" Her dismissal was what she waited for; she had prepared for it since her departure from Buffalo. That wasn't the end of it for them though. The mention of the Witness' name gave her pause as realization set in. "You're accusing me of treason."

"Aiding and abetting a terrorist at the very least, as far as I'm concerned."

"Like I give a damn about your concerns," Metcalf grumbled loud enough for all to hear. "And my replacement?"

"Is for us to know."

"Let me see him anyway."

"Susan," Stallworth said.

"It's all right, Donald," a voice called from off-screen. Metcalf waited impatiently, unsurprised at his presence in the room. The man had turned everyone against her. He had spun lies and made deals with her superiors, while threatening her subordinates. Greg Sullivan played the game very well, a rehearsed look of sadness in his eyes as he took Stallworth's position on the monitor. "My dear. You had to know this was coming."

"Oh I did, Greg," Metcalf answered. Her heart raced and her voice became louder with each word. "When I get my hands on you —"

Sullivan waved her off with a gesture. "You'll be much too busy serving a life sentence for assisting the work of a man who murdered thousands of Americans. You should have listened to me before, Susan. You needed to come out in front of this and tell the truth. Now it's too late, I'm afraid."

"Don't do this, Greg. The work we do —"

"Will continue without you, have no doubt about that. I expect things will run much better with a more open and honest leader at the helm, don't you?"

"Show me one then."

Sullivan's grin faded. "I'll miss this, Susan."

"This won't end well, Greg," Metcalf said. Her hands clenched tight to her knees. She felt her eyes fill with anger. "Especially for you."

"We'll see. Goodbye, Susan."

The screen went blank, the image of Sullivan's joy frozen in place for a long moment. Metcalf wanted to scream. She wanted to reach through the screen and take out the months of frustration that had been building up on the man who had taken advantage of the situation for his own ends. Ends, she feared, that would mean the fall of the DSA. It would be the end of all the hard work, the sacrifices, she had made for her department.

The agent to her right removed a pair of cuffs from his belt. "I have to put these on now, ma'am."

Metcalf took a deep breath. "Of course."

The cuffs slammed shut against her wrists. She bowed her head forward, staring at the metallic bracelets locking her down as easily as the two men on either side. She was trapped. Now all she could do was await her fate.

Martin slapped at the driver's shoulder. "Get us out of here."

By the time she peered up from the cuffs and faced the road ahead, the van was carrying them downtown. Blocks rushed by, the van's pace steady. Lost thoughts echoed in the bumps in the road beneath her feet. Lost opportunities at the DSA, a department she had raised from obscurity to the investigative powerhouse of the current day. She had done it for a singular reason, a lone purpose. Now that purpose was as lost as everything else. With Bunker Protocol in effect Metcalf had been able to protect those she could, but there were still pieces to put in place. She merely needed the opportunity.

Blinking lights distracted her from the back. A sedan flashed its headlights. The driver, shrouded in shadow from the distance, honked his horn. One flash of his lights was followed by another. The pattern pulled her attention.

"What the hell is that?" Metcalf asked. The two agents followed her gaze. Both left the comfort of the bench. The driver to their rear pointed to the right incessantly.

None noticed the truck run the light at the intersection of

Western and Baker. They were turning to face the driver behind them, focused on the cries pulling their attention away from what lay ahead. The truck screamed, brakes squealing and horn blaring as it barreled at them. The truck's twin cargo containers swung to the left. They blotted out the sun and darkened the interior of the van.

Metcalf closed her eyes, clutching tight to the bench beneath her, and prayed.

CHAPTER FOUR

He had forgotten to rinse the pan after cooking. It was one of those things he repeatedly failed to take into account after frying up eggs for breakfast. The schedule was always cook, eat, then head off to work. Dishes were secondary to everything else so, accordingly, they were forgotten until done by someone else.

Zac Modine left a mess in his wake wherever he went.

Leaning over the sink, he scrubbed at the pan and tore away the egg clinging for dear life. The surface refused to clean, even under the pressure of his best Brillo pad. He set the pan in the sink to soak longer and resigned himself to his failure.

Behind him, the kitchen fed into the living room on the first floor of the townhouse. Every spare corner was eaten up by furniture, most belonging to Zac's four-year-old son Alex. Toys, playsets, movies, and books littered the floor in front of the almost-vacant bookshelf where they belonged.

Zac decided to focus on the damn pan in the sink. Fixating on a single task was his way of relaxing. It held reasonably well under the pressure his position with the DSA provided him on a daily basis. Today, however, was different. His mind thought over every word struggling to break loose from his lips. When to say each one. Every inflection. Every nuance. Every movement. Every rebuttal and turn of phrase. Every scream.

Scrubbing dishes was easier for him. Not by much, but it was definitely painless compared to the conversation building in his head. He took the morning off from work. The approval came instantly from Sullivan, through the online request system Zac had put into place earlier that month. It kept the questions to a minimum, and he appreciated that more and more. People were allowed their time off—even the Head of Operational Support and Research.

Footsteps joined the chorus of curses and the splashing of dish soap on the tile. They stopped short of the kitchen, soft and fluid on the carpet. "I can't believe I overslept," Claire said with a yawn. "I don't remember hitting the pillow last... what's all this?"

Zac focused on the pan. The non-stick coating peeled away from his scrubbing. He didn't need her to see. He definitely didn't need her to comment. What he *needed* was for his wife to see the breakfast banquet laid out on the table before her. He needed her to enjoy the moment. While it lasted.

"Zac?" she asked, joining him in the room. Excitement rose in her voice. Her joy dug into his skin like sharp knives clawing for his insides.

"Breakfast."

"I see that," Claire said. She tapped the chair on the opposite side of the table. "I didn't know you were home today."

Zac placed the pan on the drying rack, then moved for the re-frigerator. He poured a small cup of orange juice before setting the beverage down in front of her waiting plate. He removed the lid, which unveiled a three-egg ham-and-cheese omelet snuggled next to three strips of bacon and twin slices of rye toast.

"I took the morning."

Zac nodded to the chair. Claire pulled it back to sit, a smile on her face. "I like this." She peered around the room, suddenly aware of the silence. "Where's Alex?"

"Your parents' place," Zac answered. He found a clean coffee cup in the back of the cupboard and emptied the remnants of the pot into the cup. He looked it over for a moment, the steam hovering beneath his lips. Then he dumped it out. He moved for the table with a glass of water instead. "Dropped him off earlier."

"Wow."

It struck him right then: the surprise at the simple act. The gesture of a shared breakfast was foreign to her. Just as foreign as his being present in the townhouse when the sun was up. He had carried the same surprise a week earlier when she'd invited him to an impromptu lunch. It was as if seeing each other was anathema to their desires. Because of him—his work, his needs. The dagger slipped deeper into his back and he slumped into the closest chair.

"That stunned to see me? I guess that says something."

Claire's hands fell on her hips and she cocked an eyebrow at her husband. "Thank you, Mr. Modine."

"Eat. Please."

Claire buttered her toast with light strokes. She used margarine, never the real stuff. Always three swipes on the bread. Clean and precise, just like her.

"I'm surprised you had time with everything at work. You're always so busy. I didn't even hear you come in last night."

He nodded, taking his time with a drink of water. He devised his own schedule both at work and at home. Since Christmas he had hidden from both, taking long meandering drives through Bethesda in the hopes of finding answers to the questions plaguing him.

Claire was right about work, however. After-action reports on a dozen cases needed filing. Reviews of the current caseload being handled by his team of researchers and analysts needed re-prioritizing. Then there was the current operation in Miami, which he had handed off to Alison Adler late last night.

She was handling the day-to-day operations in his stead. At one time, he couldn't have imagined a less likely scenario. She was a plant by Metcalf. He had distrusted her upon their very first meeting. Operations had always been his domain. It drove him, tested him, and each time he succeeded there was immense gratification.

Today, however, Adler was a godsend; she was capable of achieving the same level of operational support without the need for total control. She did it without question and without glory. For her, it was the sheer desire to do her best and never for the praise of a job well done.

Despite his reservations over her appointment to the department, Zac had let her take on more because he couldn't handle matters anymore. He needed time away from work and from home—from being Zac Modine. He needed time to *think*.

"I know," he muttered, putting his rambling thoughts aside.

"Hey," Claire said with a smile. Her hand reached for his, but he remained distant, focused on his untouched plate. "It's important. I realize that. I just like seeing you. Thank you for doing this."

Zac stopped, a large piece of egg dripping from his fork he held only inches from his lips. He let the fork go, and the utensil clanged loudly along the edge of the plate. "You don't have to..." He closed his eyes for a long moment, fighting back his first instinct. His preparation had failed him just as thoroughly as his dishwashing abilities. Six years of marriage. Two years of dating before that. Eight years spent building their lives together. Sacrificing—Claire most of all.

She had left a decent profession as a teacher to raise their son. She had also let her husband disappear for days at a time under the precept of work. She fully trusted in their love. How, then, had he rewarded her?

Morgan Dunleavy.

He still felt her lips, heard her whispers in the dark of her bedroom—their one night of passion together. He had never gone back. He wanted to, damn near did many times, but more than anything the thought of Morgan betrayed the lives he and Claire had spent the better part of a decade building together.

"You shouldn't thank me, Claire."

"Why?" she asked, confusion rippling through her baby blues. "Zac. What is it?"

Zac took a deep breath, the words resting at the tip of his tongue. They were words he should have said the moment it happened. He hadn't, and the silence had eaten at him every second since.

"Claire," he said. His vision blurred with tears. "There's something I have to tell you. Something about a woman named Morgan."

CHAPTER FIVE

Ben sucked in a deep gulp of air before slamming back into the water. Like a drunkard on a mechanical bull in a dimly lit bar, he bucked up and down, splashing the murky mix of the Miami-Dade sewage system in all directions. His fingers dug tightly into the neck of the beast beneath him as he held on for dear life. His signature Ruger was jammed between his slippery grip and the creature currently submerged in muck and a multitude of bodily fluids.

They had come to Miami to disprove the local media, of all things. It wasn't some grand conspiracy, or even a murder spree. They hunted something else entirely. Accounts of a *Crocodile Man* wandering the streets of Miami had been circulating due to some scratchy video caught by a kid's cell phone.

'People will believe anything these days,' Ben had said during the flight. Only days after almost losing his life to a rage-inducing virus, his body still ached from head to toe. His partner wasn't in much better shape, though she hadn't commented on the task ahead. She was merely grateful to leave the snow behind for some sunshine.

Ben had grumbled the entire flight. He didn't believe the stories of alligators in the New York City sewer system or Bigfoot in the Canadian outback. The Department of Special Assignments, however, had heard of much stranger things during its tenure. Zac had explained in great detail on the teleconference how pollutants in water sources had led to the creation of many different forms of life: hybrid creatures no longer quite men and definitely not completely animal in nature. Ben checked his calendar to make sure it was still January and not April—another failed joke.

There were the wendigo in Michigan, slowly trekking southward more and more each year. There were the mermaids off the Gulf Coast—not the playful *Under the Sea* singing variety. These creatures pulled people down to the bottom of the ocean just for the fun of it. As Zac had moved further into the topic, Ben had tuned him out. He simply made a mental note to always hover over public toilets going forward and to cancel his summer fishing trip.

A rush of air filled his lungs in another bout of rodeo-style fun and he caught sight of his partner. Morgan stood on the small ledge jutting from the wall, gun leveled at both Ben and his bucking captive. Impatience and frustration spread across her face. Her hand covered her mouth in an effort to block the smell. Ben scarcely noticed it anymore—his entire body was soaked in the filth flooding the underbelly of the city.

"Shoot it already!" she yelled before he submerged once more. The creature shot back up a second later, growling in anger.

"Oh, I'm sorry, Morgan," he cried, spitting God only knew how many diseases back into the water. "It's my first sewer monster!"

The Crocodile Man snapped its jaws and flailed wildly to dislodge the seated agent. Ben's fingers slid from the scales lining its neck. He crashed into the water and the waves pushed him toward the ledge. Reaching out, Ben caught a small handhold to help keep his head above the rising tide.

"It's in my eyes!" Ben cried. He tried to find his footing while scrambling to pull himself free from the river of refuse. As he collapsed along the small landing, he realized his hands were empty. His Ruger was gone. "Shit."

Maintaining his precarious position, vision dotted by the decomposing toilet paper and trash, his other hand dove back into the muck. He found no indication of his missing pistol as he leaned over the edge of the steamy liquid. What he did notice, however, was his badge and phone slip from his waterlogged breast pocket and join his gun in the sludge.

"I need a vacation," Ben muttered. His words caught in his throat as a shadow loomed over him. The creature's beady eyes gleamed with excitement. Ben wondered when its last meal had been, hoping it had eaten well enough and not that long ago.

Sharp teeth closed in on him. Ben rolled against the wall and his fingers dug around for something to use, some weapon to protect his assets — his many irreplaceable assets.

Gunfire resounded through the tunnel. Three shots echoed in the air around them. Ben blinked hard, the jaws of the creature still approaching rapidly. The frantic agent leapt back. His body slammed against the wall and he tucked tight to the brick. The excited look faded to a vacant stare in the Crocodile Man's eyes. Three holes lined the creature's back up to its neck. Blood mixed with the rest of the filth as the monster sank quietly to its end.

Morgan rushed toward him, gun firmly gripped in both hands. The growing current of the tunnel pulled the Crocodile Man down the junction and over the large drop at the end. Both paused, ready for it to return in an instant.

It never did. Morgan grabbed Ben's hand and pulled him back to his feet.

"That could have gone worse," he said, patting down his destroyed coat. He lifted the bloodstained tie to his nose, then gagged loudly at the stench.

"I doubt it," Morgan replied. She ran her hand along the wall to clean the filth gleaned from her partner's hand against the brick edifice. Ben, meanwhile, fell back to his knees at the edge of the landing. His hands dove into the sewage, desperately searching through the muck. "What are you — ?

His closed his eyes and shook his head, refusing to answer.

His coat flapped around him, and his once-white button down was now a palette of browns and blacks. His holster joined the swaying motion — empty and in full view of his curious colleague. "Sidearm?"

"And badge. And my phone," he answered. After a minute of searching he surrendered. He tried to shake his hands clean, mentally visualizing the number of showers necessary to accomplish the task.

"Zac will be pissed," Morgan said, tucking her Glock away. She started for the ladder at the far side of the tunnel.

"Somehow I'm okay with that," Ben said, trailing her closely.

"I figured." She slipped from the first rung. Ben caught her and she pushed away. Her eyes and nose lifted away from him. She pointed to the sludge trailing his every move and the flowing river beside it. "You can keep looking if you want."

"I'll pass."

"Thank God," Morgan said with a grin. She wrapped her hands into her sleeves and began the climb up to the street. "Now what?"

Ben wiped his hands off on his never-to-be-worn-again jacket. Joining it would be his black pants—a thick layer of brown-green grime had collected on it like a second skin. Above the pair of disgusted agents, the sounds of morning traffic roared through the Miami streets. He threw a deep shrug to his waiting partner.

"Breakfast?"

CHAPTER SIX

The ease of things lately surprised Morgan. After Buffalo there was a moment she had believed it would fall apart. That the partnership would break between her and Ben. So much had been said out of anger, words meant to strip them down to the core. It didn't end with the verbal either. Their wounds continued to heal after their ordeal in the Nickel City.

Ben maintained a distance after their fight. It had been instigated by an outside influence though he had failed to see it that way afterward. Morgan tried to remind him of the strange circumstances that led to their fight. It was clear in his demeanor, in the stray glances that shot her way, that he didn't quite believe her. Through it all, though, he remained by her side.

Her partner.

The term had never been a comfort to her, not until their ordeal. Now, over the three-hour flight to Dulles from Miami, she found joy in his company. It had started with their change of clothes, a necessity thanks to their visit to the sewage system of Miami-Dade County. Why Ben had kept his tie after his bath in feces remained a mystery to her, but she appreciated the levity of their hastily purchased pair of gym shorts and *Welcome to Miami* t-shirts. Ben had even gone so far as to find a rare disposable camera so they could fully embrace their roles as tourists.

With the operation completed, and thankfully no new crisis to handle in the aftermath, they managed to spend the flight conversing about their lives and relaxing in their growing relationship. Morgan discussed her last visit with her nephew at New Year's and the comics he eagerly devoured. Ben shared a new smoothie recipe he had found, which was met with rolled eyes. They shared the absurdity of their interests with a hearty laugh. Since they had dealt with a life-threatening situation before breakfast it seemed uncommonly mundane to talk about the weather, but that made its way into the conversation as well.

By the time they reached the terminal their level of comfort even extended into a shared silence. As usual, Ben seemed loathe to remain quiet for long. He pinched tight to his nose while the pair walked through the bustling terminal at Dulles.

"I still reek."

"You do," Morgan replied without looking. She glanced toward the passing crowd, noting everything from their clothes to their demeanor—including the relationships within each group. She had done it more and more frequently of late. There was no reason for the act—it was more reflex than operational.

"I mean it's *everywhere*," Ben continued, taking a whiff of his naked arm. "Whatever was in that sewer water probably mutated my DNA forever. I feel like I've grown a tail. Have I grown a tail?"

Morgan shook her head. "I'm not looking. Check out your own ass."

Ben grinned. "I'd tell you if *you* had a tail."

"Damn right you would," she said with a laugh. The ease of their friendship made her happy. The time with her family had helped as well. Things were coming together for her.

But not everything. The thought of it all stopped her. The joking and the laughing hid the fact that there was still one aspect that hung over her.

"Zac?"

Morgan's head spun to meet Ben's query. "What?"

The patient man in neon orange slowed his pace. "You make this pensive face, and there's also this pouty lip thing that happens when you're thinking about him."

"Shut up," Morgan said, slapping playfully at his shoulder.

"Deny, deny, deny."

"All right," she sighed. "I was. Now shut up."

"Hey. I respect boundaries." Ben said. A thin look passed from her, and he nodded. "Okay. *Most* boundaries."

As the crowd thinned at the terminal entrance, Morgan stopped. The two held their position near the railing while they looked down at the promenade. Couples stuck close together.

There were young lovers afraid to let each other go for a second. Then there were the married ones; they appeared more distant but the look of love was ever-present in their eyes. When she had pulled Zac into her waiting arms she had never intended for it to be more than a simple thank-you kiss. The kiss, however, had sparked a need they both shared for something other than what they had. In Morgan's case, she had nothing. It had always been her choice to live that way. Zac changed that for her. Zac, though, had a wife and a child. He had a life long before he ever met her.

"It's going to end badly, isn't it." The statement escaped before she could rein it in. Ben leaned along the railing, looking out at the same people. His soft brown eyes glowed under the overhead lights. She wondered how he kept the smile present on his face—why she couldn't see things the same way.

Ben ran his hand gently across her back. "Probably. Even the best relationships do. Makes it worth it though."

Her eyebrow creased. "Really?"

His hand fell away and he laughed. "Too fortune cookie?"

"Pretty close," Morgan remarked. The two started for the escalator and the short-term parking lot outside. "But thanks."

"Partners, right?"

Morgan took the lead down the moving stairs and chuckled. "Until you tell Metcalf about the lost sidearm. And the badge."

"Is this—?"

She stopped him. "And don't make an Obi-Wan-lecturing-Anakin-about-losing-his-lightsaber reference."

Ben fell back on his heels, shaking his head. "Quit stepping on my material. How did you—?"

"Partners, right?"

At the base of the escalator the two shifted to the right to allow the steady stream of traffic to continue. A line of vehicles were parked outside. Sunlight glistened off melting snowbanks lining the sidewalk.

"No transport?" Morgan asked. Procedure dictated internal resources be dispatched to retrieve the field team whenever they returned from a mission. It helped speed up the debriefing process. It also sure as hell saved on airport parking. It was a big plus in the budget column to someone like Director Metcalf. "You called in our arrival, didn't you?"

"When I sent in my report before takeoff," Ben replied with a nod.

Operations was rarely out of contact with the field team. It just didn't happen that way. The opposite? The field team going dark during an open mission? All the damn time. But in the home office under the auspices of Metcalf and, of course, Zac in most cases, the support team was always available. Something else was going on.

"Should we wait?"

Morgan ran her hand through her knotted hair. "For the joy of a debriefing? Honestly I'd prefer just taking another shower. Or ten."

Ben lifted the orange tee. "Exactly. Freaking sewers." He ushered his partner away from the exit, guiding her deeper into the growing chill. "Home, then?"

Scattered taxicabs waited among the row of cars and vans. Morgan headed for one farther down the line. "That sounds like heaven. How sad is that?"

Ben grimaced. "Sounds a lot better than having to stop and buy a new phone."

Morgan opened the door to the cab, then she tossed her bag inside with the flick of her wrist. "Have fun with that."

After ducking into the cab, she quickly relayed instructions to the driver before the door closed. Ben tapped the closed window, reaching for the handle. "Share one?"

Morgan rolled down the thin pane of glass. "Riley. No offense, and I mean this in the nicest way possible, but you reek."

"Seriously?"

"See you tomorrow." Morgan smiled before cutting off the cold air and his surprised stare.

The cab skirted into traffic for Bethesda. Her partner fell into the background, the stunned silence stuck on his face. When the cab merged on the interchange Morgan settled against the seat. *Home.* The thought made her smile. An afternoon off from the insanity that typically surrounded her life was just what she needed.

A quick call to Operations to notify them about the completed mission wasn't out of order. There was also the nagging question of their absence at the airport. Yet when she looked at her waiting cell phone, the number preprogrammed, she hesitated.

Zac was in Operations. He almost always was. It was like he preferred the buzzing of updating monitors to human companionship. It was like Zac preferred anything over spending time with her.

The phone returned to her pocket and she sighed. The DSA could wait one afternoon. She needed the time: to consider her next move, to finally put things to rest with her and Zac. She needed the day to finally answer the many open-ended questions in her mind—a selfish thought, but a necessary one.

Besides, what could go wrong in a single afternoon?

CHAPTER SEVEN

The hallway was empty. There were no shuffling feet or the sound of gossip being shared between colleagues. No security even greeted him upon entering the DSA warehouse to inspect his briefcase. Zac stood alone.

Forced to use his access card and the retinal scanner to gain entrance to the covert facility, Zac stepped deeper into the warehouse in a daze. His thoughts remained on the trunk of his car. More importantly, the two suitcases inside the trunk.

He hadn't been surprised by their presence. Nor had he been surprised by his wife's reaction. He had fooled around with a co-worker and all he had offered Claire in return were excuses and an overcooked omelet. At least he hadn't messed up the orange juice.

He had tried to stop talking once he'd started. Claire's cold, broken stares had begged for him to stop, but he couldn't. The burden of his secret had spilled out of him like a flood. If she understood any of what he'd said—or if she had even been listening to his apologies—it failed to slow him. All he could do was try to find the words to make sense of his mistake with Morgan.

Mistake. The word clung to his thoughts, demanding clarification—begging for accuracy. He had enjoyed their time together. After everything—the doubt and the self-recrimination—part of him wondered if it had been meant to happen. Had the affair been a long-ignored course correction?

It didn't matter anymore. He had made the choice to tell his wife and paid the price. With each step down the vacant hall, the future plagued him. What came next for him? For Claire? He wanted to be there for her, to ease her pain, though he knew he never could. Then there was Alex. What would happen to him? How could Zac explain any of it to his son?

He paused at Metcalf's office. The door was shut and locked; it wasn't the strangest thing in the world, but the fact that he hadn't seen his superior in days or that her personal assistant Stephanie Atwater wasn't at her desk either was something he could no longer ignore. Detail snapped into focus for the distracted analyst. No lights filled the waiting area to the director's office. Computer cables dangled without connection, and the terminals had been pulled from their stations.

Voices rang out behind him. The sound carried through the void of the corridor, originating from the Research room at the heart of the DSA. Zac trailed the noise, then skidded to a halt in the shadows of the waiting area as a lone figure rushed in the opposite direction.

Allison Adler cradled her tablet, the same way she always did. She pulled back her straggly brown hair and tucked it behind her left ear. Without concern for onlookers, she powered down to the far end of the corridor and ducked around the corner.

Curiosity won out over caution, and Zac pursued her. All thoughts of Claire and Morgan, the eternal debate, dissipated as new questions arrived. He passed the hub, glancing inside only to notice the crowd of analysts gathered near the back of the room.

Zac shook his head. His brisk pace closed the distance with the woman. When he rounded the corner Adler was out of sight. The door to the janitor's closet—the only door available in the abbreviated corridor—was already shut. What the hell was she doing? There was nothing relevant inside. He quickly opened the door.

"Huh?" Shelving lined the walls of the cramped space. The no-windows rule of the converted warehouse pertained to the closet as much as the rest of the building. Zac inched inside, pawing at spray bottles and spare mops for the janitorial staff. "Adler?"

Gone. The how of it all eluded him, but so did many things these days. She had entered the room only scant seconds before him. There were no places to hide, no connecting chambers, and no ventilation access other than the small floor vent in the center

Where did she go?

The question followed him back to the Research hub, the largest room in the facility. Cubicles in long rows comprised the majority of the space. Office supplies and a spare coffee machine sat on a long table to the right of the entrance. Monitors decorated the far side, objectives and priorities emblazoned in multi-colors with names attached to each project. It was his design, and one that worked for that varied tasks which constantly changed and evolved.

It appeared to be doing both today. At the center of the crowd gathered beneath the monitors, Greg Sullivan continued to address the crowd. Whispers rose from the outskirts, though they were quieted down by colleagues trying to catch every word spoken by the man in the tan sweater vest and khakis.

"What's going — ?"

A woman holding a pencil with a troll head at the end raised a finger to her lips, silencing Zac's question. Glances shifted his way from the surrounding analysts and he waved sheepishly. No one returned his greeting, not that he expected any from his colleagues. He may have been their direct superior, but he would never actually be superior to them in any way that mattered. They recognized his place in the hierarchy, yet they failed to respect him.

Zac crossed his arms and shuffled away from the others for the comfort of a nearby desk. He leaned along the edge, searching the room for the field team, for anyone else in a place of authority. Instead of locating Riley, or even Morgan, he found a line of agents carrying firearms and jackets emblazoned with the DSA logo on their chest. He recognized none of them as internal. The only friendly face was the man speaking.

"Now I know all this might be shocking to you," Sullivan said. His gaze drifted between analysts, never settling on a single one — he used his political experience to play to the audience. "I know you've been working your collective butts off on high-priority cases all over the country. Your work on these is not in question. Additionally, your dedication and drive are not to be diminished by this blow. You didn't know. I didn't either. But it cannot continue."

Zac's brow furrowed in confusion. Of all days to come in late, it had to be today. Sullivan spoke in riddles to him. Metcalf's name was mentioned in whispered breaths by those around him. The field team came up as well—though with more surprise in his colleague's voices.

He completely forgot somehow. Riley and Morgan were in Miami, working a case. It was an open operation, yet the entire staff ignored their tasks. Who was monitoring communications? Who was passing along useful intel to assist any priority situations? What was happening at the DSA, and why hadn't Sullivan informed him?

"Effective immediately I have been promoted to Director of the DSA," Sullivan announced. Few gasps escaped at the news. Some people clapped in response. Zac remained silent. "Susan Metcalf has been removed from her position over this affair. It is not what I wanted. But it is necessary to move forward. There were things we should have done, decisions that can't help but be viewed as mistakes. The decisions we are making today are steps to return to the good work you've always done and will continue to do."

Bellbrook. Grissom. So many others. Zac had reported on them all, sided with Sullivan on each and every one. The news stung, regardless. Metcalf had recruited him, brought him to the DSA and trusted him to shape the department to the best of his ability. What had changed in her? What had changed in *him* over their time together? Somehow his trust had shifted to doubt over time. Recently it had turned to outright objections over her choices.

"This change will take time," Sullivan continued. "For now, however, operations have been suspended in the field. As for in this office, we will be working together to wind down our open caseload for the time being in order to refocus our priorities."

"What?" Zac asked, the question louder than intended. It went ignored by those around him, and it was unheard by the man addressing the crowd. Was Sullivan reassigning him, removing him from his position? Was that why Sullivan had failed to mention this little change prior to making it known to the whole department?

Is that why Adler disappeared?

"Now I know how this sounds," Sullivan said, hands raised to quiet the growing grumbles from the crowd. "Like I've been buttering you up just to pull the dinner plate from you. That's not how I see it, though. The fact is, the DSA had a chink in its armor. At the very top. How far down the crack goes is what we need to determine. Today, I want you to focus on closing out our current workload and keeping the quality and efficiency you've always brought to the table."

He showcased the line of agents along the wall at his side. "Meanwhile, our new Security Division will be working up an interview list. When they call your name, they'll be asking you a few routine questions. It will help us see what we could have done to avoid this situation. Maybe something you noticed during the old regime but were afraid to pass on. When that is all said and done, we will get back to work. Faster and harder than ever. I can't do this without you."

Concerns waned from the audience. The charm behind his words, the perfect inflection, and the glimmer in his eye locked every single member of the team in place. Sullivan worked the masses, the consummate politician.

He clapped his hands together. "Now let's get to it."

The crowd dispersed, hypnotic to the man's commands. Five steps in, the whispers began and grew to full discussions until they were silenced by the pacing security personnel. Analysts sat at their desks, eyes locked on their screens.

Zac pushed through the audience for Sullivan, who retreated for the stairs to the lower level alone. "Deputy Director! I mean… Director."

Sullivan paused and glanced back. "Ah, Zac. Just the man I was hoping to see."

He sidled next to the tech and led him down the stairs. Zac stopped in the base of the steps. His arms crossed and he leaned lightly along the cold concrete of the opposite wall.

"What is going on, sir?"

"Exactly what you heard," Sullivan answered. He pointed to Operations down the corridor. "Walk with me."

"Shouldn't I be helping close things out?" Zac asked, not moving from his position.

Sullivan shook his head. "I need you to keep working on our project."

"The Wellspring."

From what Zac had been told, the Wellspring was an artifact

of immense power. It was also incredibly important to his superior. Its recovery was a top priority, though Zac knew little more than what he had been told on the subject. Metcalf was aware of its location, or was closer than any of them to finding the priceless tool. It had been another secret kept from them by the former director.

"Things are moving quickly," Sullivan said. Zac pushed from the wall, joining him on their slow walk. "With the Wellspring in the open we need to make sure it is found by our people."

"Metcalf's files are—"

"Your only priority," he finished. Sullivan stopped. His tongue ran the length of his teeth. "Find it, Zac. The department is counting on you. *I* am counting on you."

They passed the plaques of the fallen soldiers, lost in the service to the DSA. Zac's gaze locked on Grissom's name, and then on Ruth's. Both had died recently, each one a blow to the department's morale.

"I'd like to know about the field team first, sir. You didn't mention them."

Sullivan's brow furrowed. "Why, it was the very first thing I mentioned. I'm surprised you missed it."

"I came in late."

Sullivan nodded. "Personal time. I remember seeing the request. How is Claire?"

"Fine. She's fine," Zac replied, picturing the suitcases waiting for him in his car. His mistake had cost him his home and his family. He couldn't lose anything else. "The team, sir? Riley? Morgan?"

"They're being brought in," Sullivan said, his eyes cold.

"Routine questions?"

"No, Zac," the newly installed director admitted. "Much like Susan, they've been working against the better interests of both the DSA and this great country."

"What?" the tech exclaimed. "What are you saying?"

"I'm doing what has to be done, Zac. You have to understand that." Sullivan squeezed his shoulder. "They are being detained."

"On what charges?"

"Treason," Sullivan said. "They are traitors to the DSA and they will pay the price for their betrayal."

CHAPTER EIGHT

He had prepped all week. Not an easy task considering the amount of people searching for him. Lincoln MacKenzie, however, always did enjoy a challenge. Former superiors and colleagues recalled his anal-retentive nature for stockpiling shit for a rainy day.

It sure as hell was pouring now.

He had gathered the necessary equipment quickly. He still had contacts from his army days, men who had served in the most dangerous locations in the world with him. They never asked questions. To them, he was family and you did what you could for family, no matter what the favor. This meant weapons, explosives, burner phones, and more. One even offered an old junker from his garage, barely street-worthy, but enough for the few errands necessary. Another wished to join in a more active role and lend a helping hand. Lincoln drew the line there.

This was for him alone. There would be no cavalry, no great rescue at the eleventh hour. The mission would succeed or fail on his watch, and every decision was his burden to bear. Well, not quite his alone.

"Sullivan has made his move."

The voice echoed throughout the emptiness of the room. Lincoln wondered how long the man had been standing there, though he didn't bother to turn to face his colleague. He continued to squint through the lenses of the binoculars and stare across the brightly lit sky at the warehouse set apart from the main strip in downtown Bethesda. A clear sight line of the target had attracted Lincoln to the property, the lack of eyes on him nothing more than a bonus.

Traffic in and out of the warehouse was minimal. Once they entered the premises, employees stayed for the duration of their shifts. A typical stint ran for at least eight hours depending on the day. It gave him enough time to go over the plan once more before the end.

"Did you hear me, Lincoln?" The Witness reached the staging tables positioned in the center of the room. A lone lamp lit the area; they kept their footprint as limited as possible to avoid detection. The office had once held a telemarketing firm, though it had gone under months earlier. High rents kept qualified tenants from biting, which had left the space abandoned and worth the risk in occupying.

It was safer than the tenement on the Upper East Side—his previous safehouse. The neighbors had been growing more concerned with his comings and goings, nervous from the increasing patrols after his recent run-in with the police.

"And Metcalf?" Lincoln asked.

He lowered the binoculars and returned to the waiting table and his guest. The Witness' eyes remained hidden behind his opaque glasses, but his head bowed in response. "I'm afraid she's been taken off the board."

Dead? Was such a feat possible? When he had met the brusque director she had immediately commanded his respect. It had surprised him—not because she was a woman or because of her manner of dress and mandatory heels, but because he had imagined Grissom would be the one running the show. When she had taken charge of his first operation, when she had put him in the field, trusting him to make the call on the ground, she had proved her worth to him.

The Witness had confirmed his worst fears. This wasn't a game anymore. Lives were on the line, and he had to make sure no more fell if he could help it.

"It's time, Lincoln."

The Witness' original timetable had depended on the actions of others. Though it had once been flexible, now there was a ticking clock. Sullivan had made the first move. He would only have done so if pushed to act. It was time to push back.

The Witness shuffled aside metallic discs occupying the nearest table. Lincoln reached out and stopped him. "Careful with the equipment." He pulled the discs from the table and delicately placed them inside one of a pair of duffel bags. "I'd rather not have these explosives go off accidentally."

"Explosives?"

"You asked me to prepare for any situation. This is me being prepared."

The Witness nodded, and he waited for Lincoln to set the bags aside before proceeding to lay out the paperwork clutched in his hand. Blueprints of the four-story warehouse sprawled the length of the folding table.

"I've never seen these schematics before," Lincoln admitted. There were spaces he had never envisioned in the warehouse. He noted a number of choke points along the basement level, but more importantly he noticed new opportunities for infiltration that didn't include the main entrance.

"Does that surprise you?"

Nothing the Witness did anymore surprised Lincoln. He held all the answers before the question could even be asked, recognized all the cards in the deck before they were even dealt. It grated Lincoln, but he had grown accustomed to the back and forth.

Instead, he focused on the building's layout. Something stuck out to him: there was an unseen hatch on the first level. It led to the exterior of the building, yet also ran up the entire back wall of the structure. It was almost like an emergency exit, yet completely concealed from the occupants.

"I'll head in here." Lincoln pointed at the blueprints. He was aware of the closet next to it. It was a relatively quiet area on the first level. He would be able to better gauge traffic once inside. "Six hours from now."

The Witness didn't bother to check the time against his own. He merely nodded in agreement. "Minimal personnel will be in the area. You will have a clear path to your objective."

The confidence behind the statement frustrated Lincoln despite his relative ease at accepting it. The Witness understood things on a level Lincoln never could. Where each variable brought a number of questions to the forefront, the Witness only saw conclusive data. Lincoln was forced to trust in the information; he had to trust in the man telling it like it already happened.

The spectacled gentleman read his silent thoughts. "I swore

answers for you, Lincoln. You'll have them."

Lincoln grimaced. "After I jump through hell for you."

"I didn't create the situation," the Witness replied. "Just try to remember that."

"Oh, I'm trying."

No matter the story told or the blame laid elsewhere, the suited figure had had a hand in creating their current situation. He had put Lincoln on this path the moment the grieving agent had been dispatched to bring the enigmatic figure in for his involvement in the Bellbrook affair. The Witness had strung him along, forced him into a confrontation with his past in Des Moines, and now?

Now the Witness was leading Lincoln into the lion's den with little more than a hope and a prayer.

"Sullivan needs to be stopped," the Witness continued. "Before he discovers the whereabouts of the Wellspring."

Stopped. It held more meaning to the ex-soldier. What the Witness truly meant was killed. Sullivan's death ensured a successful mission. All Lincoln had to do was pull the trigger. Just like always; it was the same directive decreed by Metcalf in his hunt for the stranger at his side. The only thing he ever did in life was take it.

"Why is this thing so important?" he asked, struggling to stay on task.

The Witness rubbed at his forehead, his shadow looming over the table between them. "Imagine being in the room when the personal computer became a reality. Think about what it must have been like to work in the lab with Alexander Fleming when he discovered penicillin. The Wellspring made these events and discoveries—these and so many more—possible. It is what has caused our rapid progression as a society."

"Why?"

The Witness smiled. "That, my reluctant friend, is the question no one ever thinks to ask. Why help us at all? Why provide the means for us to evolve beyond our rudimentary knowledge of science and technology?"

Lincoln's jaw clenched. "You know the answer, don't you."

The Witness tapped the frame of his glasses, the scars beneath poking out for an instant before he hid them once more. "I've seen how this ends, Lincoln. No one should have to live through what comes next. You cannot conceive the horrors Greg Sullivan helps to unleash if he should attain the Wellspring."

"I'll stop him."

The Witness left the table and headed for the edge of the room. He stared away from Lincoln, toward the warehouse in the distance. "You have to, Lincoln," he called. "There can be no hesitation. When the time comes you must pull the trigger."

Lincoln's head bowed. "I... Let's go through it again."

There were only six hours left until it was time to choose a side. Was he loyal to the Witness or to the DSA? Was he a taker of life, or a protector of those he cared for? He leaned over the blueprints, the shadow spreading across the table threatening to swallow him whole. "One more time."

CHAPTER NINE

Was it wrong to be in love with something as simple as good water pressure? Morgan dared anyone to say otherwise. Currently, she considered her shower her best friend in the world. The blasting water cleansed her dark skin of the residue real or imagined from her time in the Miami sewers. Heaven held nothing on the sensation, which felt almost like shedding her skin and starting fresh.

If only everything was that easily accomplished.

The rushing water faded with a twist of the handle. Small drips rhythmically fell from her athletic frame. She reached for the warm comfort of the towel resting on the sink. The soft cotton wrapped around her like a blanket and provided her a moment of pure pleasure against the cold air that infiltrated her apartment. She wanted to hold that serenity, anything to keep her uncertainty from creeping back in. She promised to take the day, to keep work out of sight and out of mind. With work came the eventual interaction with *him*.

Zac.

Morgan shook her head, refusing to drag herself out of her bliss. She refused to picture him waiting for her in the bedroom or imagine the way the light from the street outside beamed off his body.

A growl escaped her—frustration at the whole series of events. Zac's shadow echoed against everything in the apartment. The few hours they'd spent post coital was the best time she had had in years. Zac had made all the mistakes from her past disappear into the background. Now his image haunted her almost as much.

The towel fell to the tile. She moved for the dresser at the far end of the bedroom. She pulled loose the few clean clothes remaining: a simple workout outfit, gray sweatpants, and a red tank top that made her look phenomenal in front of the mirror. They were another comfort necessary in her eyes for the day ahead.

A day away from work. A day away from people and hang-ups. She'd earned it. With so much dedication to the job, little time existed for the upkeep of her personal life. Even her apartment had suffered in her absence. Overdue laundry piled high in the corner of multiple rooms. Months-old magazines and a dozen unfinished books were stacked on the nightstand and her coffee table. Who knew what remained in the fridge. *Is there anything in there not weeks past its expiration date?*

Zac could wait. *Everything could wait*, she thought, scanning herself in the mirror. She brushed her hair back, though the ends fought against her efforts. She pulled the naturally curly mess into a simple tail at the back. Nothing impressive, since there was no one around to impress. She was on her own for the night. It sounded as wonderful as the shower had been. A movie night and some takeout. Something light called for on both fronts.

Energized, Morgan started for the living room and her phone. She snagged the charging device from the dining room table before heading to the adjacent room. Her phone nearly fell from her hand when she caught sight of a shadow perched at the end of the couch.

"Who's there?" she called into the darkness. Her gun rested on the end table near the entryway, no more than fifteen feet away. She silently cursed herself for not keeping it closer. Her hand tucked the phone behind her back. She crept ahead, slow and cautious. "Step into the light so I can see you."

The shadow remained still. Two eyes of fierce blue shone in the darkness of the living room. She had only ever seen eyes like that on one man's face. Her jaw slackened, and words escaped her as quickly as her resolve. The chiseled face. The broad shoulders. Familiar enough, but his eyes connected it all for her.

They belonged to only one man, though she found it hard to believe. He was dead. She had watched him die.

"It can't be," she uttered, the words barely audible. Beyond question, beyond doubt, it was him. The man who had saved her from her lowest point. The man who had recruited her for the DSA. He stood from the couch, the frame groaning at the release of so much weight. His eyes beamed as bright as she remembered them as he stood before her.

"Grissom?"

CHAPTER TEN
Four Years Ago

Calling the place a hole was an understatement. It was more than simply dilapidated or decrepit. It went beyond such description, beyond any single word as each pretended it was possible to change: that hope existed in such a space. That it held some redemptive quality if only it were cleaned up or refurbished.

Altano's Pub held no hope. Morgan had chosen the establishment because of that. The bar was hidden in the Midwest without a clear sign to guide patrons inside. How the place found regulars was a modern miracle—not of the walking-on-water variety. It was more of the cast-out-into-the-desert-for-forty-years situation if relaying on a biblical level. Sodom and Gomorrah must have been paradises in comparison.

It had taken her weeks to find the bar while driving aimlessly across the country. Tears had become permanent residents in her eyes. They flowed freely with each glance in the rearview mirror at those she had left behind—those locked in her memory. Her nephew. Her sister-in-law. Her brother, most of all. They had been joined by her medical license and any career dreamed of since the age of three, playing doctor with her stuffed animals. Her mistakes had come with a hefty price.

Working in the bar acted as penance for them. When she had crossed Nebraska, stumbling across two lanes of highway in a drunken stupor only to crash her car in a ditch, she had located Altano's. The owner-slash-barkeep-slash-cook-slash-pretty-much-everything-else had nothing to offer but a cot above the garage out back and a job.

She accepted both, taking the man's hand but never offering anything else of herself. Not a smile. Not a name. Not a past. She didn't exist. Merely an employee, she dealt drinks and passed along tasteless, overcooked bar fare. The owner never asked, never cared to inquire.

Few in the regular crowd ever bothered to question her past. They laughed, they cajoled, and they screamed at sports on television—when the static broke through the trees surrounding the place—but names disappeared and personal attributes faded. It was just the way Morgan needed it to be, needed everything to be.

She couldn't face the deaths she'd caused to save the life of her brother. It had been the right choice in the matter, she swore up and down when alone on her cot, staring at the stains seeping from the leaky roof above her head. It was the right decision, the only one she was able to live with. Ty hadn't been able to accept it, though, and his reaction cost her everything.

Six months she spent at the bar. In the mornings she washed the floors after a jog up to the highway and back. Her car was long gone. It had been scrapped after her crash. During her morning run, though, she would cross the street to where it happened. It was the final resting place of her former life.

The afternoons generally brought out a few of the locals, and by evening the flow was so steady hours passed in a heartbeat. Laughing and joking. Never connecting and never making eye contact. Hands sometimes swung in her direction in the late hours, some landed on her body for a quick feel, but few remained for fear of the loud snapping of fingers and wrists. She was brutal in her justice, maintaining her privacy no matter the query asked by the rare stranger to her hideaway.

She preferred the rigid schedule. It gave her little time to think, and little time to see the ragged nature of her appearance. Morgan was as lost as her past and she needed the distance, prayed it would never end; that the pain never returned.

Then he walked in the place.

He was clean-shaven with a neatly trimmed haircut. He wore a tight shirt, accentuating his strapping physique. He carried a soldier's stance, tall and proud. She tried to turn away, did everything but run to the kitchen for orders nowhere near ready, all to avoid any contact with the stranger among them. His eyes locked on hers and refused to give up on pulling her in. They were sharp and blue in the dim haze of the bar—through cigar smoke and random fumes mixing with the poorly ventilated air. They were electric, charged, and vibrant.

He didn't speak to the pondering crowd drawn by his arrival. Nods were offered to a few, the tipping of hats in reply; however, the figure continued to the bar and to her. When he perched on the stool, a smile cracked through the surface.

Morgan wiped the counter. "What will it be?"

"A job."

His voice was strong and confident. It unsettled her. She tried not to look at him and scrubbed more diligently. "Not hiring as far as I know. I can put in a word with the owner, though he doesn't give a crap about my opinion, truth be told."

"I meant a job for you," he clarified. "I could use someone with your skills on my team."

Morgan shuffled back, a nervous chuckle on her lips. The dirt on the counter remained, despite her efforts. "I have a job."

"I think you can do better."

She started for the back, tossing the rag to the floor. "This has been fun, pal, but—"

The man stood and shot a hand out, stopping her short of her escape. "Morgan."

The name forced her to pause, forced her to reconsider. "How?"

"It's time to get back to work, Morgan," he continued, his voice drowned out by the skipping music from the out-of-warranty jukebox and the murmurs of the overweight women at the end of the bar hungrily staring at the newcomer. "Time to start living again. What do you say?"

"Who the hell are you?"

"The name's Grissom. I think you're going to like what I have to offer."

He pointed to the door, and she followed without a word. What he was offering was a second chance, a way back to the light, one she never believed possible. For six months she had hidden away from the opportunity, penance for her sins, but in five minutes he had won her over.

Running wasn't the answer. Redemption came from deeds, not in hiding. Jacob Grissom had given her that chance, a way to move past the sins of war, the mistakes of the past.

It had been a way to start again.

She owed everything to him. And now, he had come to collect.

CHAPTER ELEVEN

He had died.

It was as simple as that. Grissom, during a routine operation with the DSA, had stumbled into the laboratory of Oliver Blake and had been exposed to a lethal virus of unknown origin or type. Rather than risk containment breach to the outside, Grissom had locked the lab down—sentencing himself to a lonely and excruciating end.

It had happened. That was a fact.

So how was he sitting on her couch?

"Is it really you?" She inched into the living room, bare feet sliding through thick shag carpet. He remained in shadow. A dull hum rose in the background. "How can you be—?"

"Stay back."

His voice staggered her. Sharp and cold, almost mechanical, the words cut through the air. Morgan paused, hesitant in her approach.

"Grissom?"

"Back away now, Morgan," Grissom answered. "I won't say it again."

A slight nod escaped her. She backpedaled to the edge of the room to give him some distance. What was he hiding? What changed in him from the last time they had spoken, laughed, and enjoyed each other's company? For months she had believed him to be dead, fought to continue the work the way he taught her; she had pushed herself to take on more in the hopes of doing him proud.

Now he was here. It overwhelmed her, heat rising from her chest. "This..." Her hands ran through her hair before tightening the tail in back. "This is incredible. We should be celebrating!"

The words flew out of her, panicked and confused, but joyous over the reunion. He had saved her life and she had never thanked him for it, never said a word as to how much the act meant to her.

Grissom, however, made no motion.

An uncontrolled smile grew on her face. "Come on, Jake! You're not dead! It's—"

"No thanks to you."

"What?" Morgan pressed forward, unconcerned with his stern warning. "That's… that's not true. I fought with Metcalf. I tried to save you."

The shadows receded. Grissom's hands fell to his sides, leaving his body unobstructed. "Do I look saved to you?"

"My God," she uttered. From the seated position he appeared just as he always had. Strong, muscular, and virile. The perfect soldier. Standing before her, he loomed inches over her six-foot-three frame.

It was only the start of the changes in Grissom. Shining blue orbs pierced the darkness of the apartment—the same electrifying shade she had first noted years earlier. Closer inspection revealed that to be anything but the case. His blue irises shifted and focused like miniature cameras, eyelids only blinking to retain the image like a memory file. When they disconnected from a focal point, both scanned in uniform fashion: right to left, top to bottom, appearing to capture every nuance in the environment.

Larger cybernetic implants were positioned on muscle clusters. His arms, legs, and torso were augmented, fitted with wires that fed from a central processing unit close to his heart. His skin was patchy. Deep veins of blue and purple pulsed, channeling vital fluids—all visible for her observation. This wasn't Grissom, not completely, but a patchwork of a man. A mechanical construct.

"Who did this to you?" Morgan asked, struggling to find her voice. "Nanotech grafts. Cybernetic implants. I've never seen anything like this before. This isn't a RadioShack special we're talking about here."

Silence answered her. His hands hovered close to his belt, over twin pistols she had failed to notice on his person. She had been so enraptured at the miracle of Grissom's return, she had forgotten the potential threat he presented.

Her sidearm sat with her badge on the end table across the room. It was only fifteen feet away, though it may as well have been five hundred feet for all it mattered.

The quiet unnerved her. "The silent treatment doesn't suit you."

"And sarcasm never suited you."

It was an astute observation, one learned from years in the field together. She had always been the serious one on the team, always working the case over any and all interaction. She had changed since his loss. She blamed Riley for the sarcasm.

Ben. Sudden concern ripped through her. Riley deserved to know about this, about Grissom's return, and what it meant for them going forward.

"Who did this to you?" she said again.

"*You* did, Morgan," Grissom replied. A pistol settled into his right hand, though it was still leveled at the ground. "When you left me behind."

"That's not—"

A shot boomed out, the bullet soaring mere inches from her right side. Morgan tucked close, hands over her ears and a scream held on her lips.

"I gave you everything," Grissom continued. "A life. A purpose."

Plaster smoked along the column separating the small eating nook from the kitchen proper. It snapped Morgan back in full. Her terror was replaced by fury. "And I would have done anything to save you! I fought for you!"

The conversation echoed in her mind. The struggle with not only Ruth and Lincoln but with Metcalf, who had been three thousand miles away and fully detached from the events of that fateful morning. Morgan had promised success if only given the chance to save Grissom. Metcalf had refused. She had been right to do so. It had taken months to reconcile that fact, to accept the circumstances as they stood.

"But, I was wrong," she said. She took a sharp breath, swallowing the anger and remembering the pain of his loss. Her brown eyes softened and she reached out to him. "You broke protocol. You walked into Blake's lab against orders and breached containment. We… I didn't have a choice."

Grissom stepped away. His cold, exacting stare refused to accept her words. Tears stung her eyes and she swiped at them. She wiped away the memory with them and it left her with only the burning question from that day, yet to be answered.

"Why? Why did you go in there?"

"Orders."

"There were none! Nothing in our briefing—"

"You're wrong," Grissom snapped, grip tightening on his weapon. "I *did* have orders."

"From Metcalf?"

"Susan?" he scoffed. Disdain and disbelief rolled into one. "She was clueless, just like the rest of you."

The accusation stung, and a chill washed over her skin. "Then spell it out for me."

He leaned close, cold eyes piercing. "The DSA? Your so-called second chance? Nothing more than a puppet."

"And you pulled the strings?"

"Among others," he said with a smirk. "Shifting assets. Smuggling intel. Secondary and tertiary objectives embedded into operations to fill their needs."

"Who?"

"They call themselves the Trust."

"This Trust—they sent you here?"

Grissom shook his head, his gears winding with each turn. "Sullivan."

Morgan nearly fell as the name slipped from his lips. Gregory Sullivan. Deputy Director of the DSA. Grissom's replacement and another plant from the so-called organization controlling the department's actions. Worse, *her* actions. He had been twisting her ideals, manipulating her purpose for some unknown reason. He was playing an unseen game from behind the scenes and using her as their pawn.

Were there more traitors in their midst? Was anyone who they said they were at the DSA?

"Sullivan found me at Blake's that day. He and a team posed as the CDC backup you called in for cleanup and containment. He pulled me apart and pieced me back together like a damn jigsaw puzzle. Turned me into this, then put me in Asset Control. Frozen. Time stopped for me. Until today."

Morgan wanted to scream. Her body begged for a release of the tension piled on her with Grissom's every confession. She didn't know anything anymore. She had failed to consider so much about the life she'd led at the DSA. She had believed in the organization because of Grissom. It was all because of the ideal he instilled in her, the faith to carry out the job.

Everything he had said, every lesson drilled into her, had been a lie. Right from the start.

"Jake," she said. "I don't... I can't know what you've been through, but—"

"No. You can't."

She nodded, understanding the sentiment. This wasn't why he had come, nor why he stood like a damn sentry in her living room. This wasn't about his glorious return. He hadn't come to hear her explanation for what happened.

Grissom came for something else.

"Why?" The question fell out before she could contain it. "Why are you here, then? What does Sullivan want you to do?"

"To make you an offer. A chance to stand with him."

And against the DSA? Against Ben? Her arms fell across her chest. "If I don't?"

"Morgan."

"Tell me."

His left hand extended, open and empty. "This doesn't have to be a fight, Morgan. Take the offer and my hand with it. Work with me again. Do some good."

Morgan shook her head. "I thought I was. I trusted you, Jake. I won't make that mistake again."

The left receded and the right rose with his gun in hand. "Dammit, Morgan."

"I'm sorry, Jake. I made my choice. I know where I stand."

"I know," he admitted. "I always did. That's why I'm here and not someone else. It had to be me."

"Why?"

"To do what you never did for me." She stared down the barrel of Grissom's weapon. Eyes once brilliant blue turned red. "To make the end quick and clean."

CHAPTER TWELVE

"You don't have to do this, Jake." Morgan said, trying to push through his cold stare. "Please. Let me help you."

A knock at the door rang out. Grissom's gaze shifted toward the sound, but his hand never moved. The knock echoed through the apartment. Morgan's heart leaped in her chest.

"Ma'am?" a voice called through the door. "It's the police."

Oh, no. Someone heard the shot and called for help.

Grissom scanned the front door. His posture tightened. She tried to grab his attention.

"I want to help you," she said. He refused to look, focused on the door. "You have to know that."

"Send them away, Morgan," Grissom grumbled. "Do it now or so help me—"

"No threats," she snapped, unafraid. Threats served no one in their current situation. She held her hands up and open for him to see before starting for the door.

"From there."

"Great." She took a sharp breath to swallow her terror, then threw on an unseen smile. "Everything's fine here! Really... the TV was too loud!"

"Open the door, ma'am," the officer replied. "We need to see you to confirm your safety."

Grissom gave her a cold stare.

"Can't help you there, Officer," Morgan said. "I'm not exactly dressed for the occasion."

The sound of muttering carried under the thin apartment door. "We're coming in, ma'am."

Grissom's eyes widened. "Don't."

"Don't!"

The door crashed into the apartment. The two officers rushed into the room with guns raised. Morgan backed away from the entrance, pivoting for the counter and her waiting sidearm. She pulled it down with her as she dove for cover. Her right side smashed against the carpet and she rolled beneath the kitchen counter. Both officers, young and confident, stopped short of the living room, their eyes plastered on the over-sized target before them. Grissom's eyes glowed red in the darkness.

Morgan pulled the gun from its holster, screaming at the frozen pair. "Get down! Get the hell down!"

"What is—?"

The other was more muted, only able to utter a single word. "God—"

Two shots rang out, silencing both officers. They happened so quickly she didn't see Grissom's fingers pinch against the triggers to greet their guests. A single shot from each weapon found its target. The officers were dead before their bodies hit the ground of the shallow entryway.

"No!" she exclaimed at the blatant disregard for life. He was no longer Jacob Grissom in her eyes. She jumped up from behind the counter and unloaded four shots center mass into the behemoth. Each one found its mark. Four bullets, kill shots each and every one; at least, they would have been when it came to a normal man.

Unfortunately, Grissom was not normal. Not anymore.

"I never wanted this for you, Morgan. I told you what would happen."

Morgan made her way to her feet, then slowly backed toward the shattered door and the dead men. She stared at the result of her assault. Grissom remained standing, four holes through his flak jacket and the flesh beneath. No blood poured out. A number of wires had been clipped in the assault. They sprayed black fluid at his feet for an instant before closing up. He holstered the pistol in his right hand, then ripped the wires free. Replacements grew, reconnecting with intact circuits and functions.

"That's not good."

"Damn you, Morgan. This should have been quick!"

Morgan dove over the dead men and rolled into the hallway. Bullets cut above her. Momentum carried her into the opposite wall, her legs kicking to escape Grissom's line of sight. Air was pushed out of her lungs from the impact on the floor, as her ribs were only barely healed from recent injuries. She refused to think about the pain or the dead men in her entryway. She refused to think about anyone on the opposite side of the wall across from her apartment. All she could do was hope the place was empty during the waning afternoon hours. She pushed aside the potential loss of life, allowing only one thought to take over — the only one that mattered.

Run.

Morgan crawled rapidly as a fresh barrage shattered the plaster above. He aimed high again to force her to the ground. She pushed ahead; her short breaths fought against her frayed nerves.

Move your ass.

The moment the gunfire paused, she kicked to her feet. She barreled down the hall in a full run. She needed cover. There were six apartments on the floor. Any one of them could have provided her with an escape, but they also allowed too much potential for collateral damage. What she truly needed was to get out of the building. *And then what?* It didn't matter. One step at a time. The hall was clear — that was all she could have hoped for at the moment.

The elevator rested at the end of the corridor. It was too far, with little chance the car waited patiently on her floor. The stairwell to its left, however, gave her a clear exit. If she could reach it in time. Loud crunches and the creaking of worn floorboards echoed over the pounding of her chest. Grissom moved toward her, each step lumbering, every one announced to spike her anxiety.

Just a few damn seconds. Push it, Morgan. Go.

The stairwell just out of reach. She turned back, hoping for more time. Grissom stood in her shattered doorway, a looming shadow that seemed to carry the length of the hall. His eyes, still magnificently bright, beamed toward her. His took aim. All he needed was one bead on her.

She refused to give it to him. She leapt with everything she had toward the stairs, putting the bulk of her weight against the push bar at the center of the metal door. Air swirled near her hair as a single bullet cut past her.

Bright lights welcomed her to the stairwell. She crashed along the landing hard, then fumbled forward toward the edge. She snatched the railing and held on for dear life. Afraid her legs would surrender to the strain, Morgan started down the stairs. The steps were cold to the touch and the fleeing agent suddenly wished socks were part of her ensemble.

She took the steps two at a time, holding tight to the railing to keep her balance. The last thing she needed was to twist an ankle. Rushing down three flights of stairs in a matter of seconds, Morgan pulled open the door to the lobby and fell to her knees on the carpet. Deep breaths filled her. She tried to slow her pulse and relax her frantic body.

By the time she peered up and around the lobby of the complex, five shadows had converged on her. The five figures, all male, were heavily armed and clearly not in the mood for a conversation.

"DSA!" one of the men bellowed as he moved for her.

"What?" she asked. The man's jacket was deep blue, matching the other four. All carried the same logo embroidered on the left breast—a logo reading three distinct characters.

DSA

"Don't move!" another agent shouted. Behind them, a number of residents backed away in a hurry, rushing for the nearest exit.

"You're under arrest!" the first agent yelled, sidearm aimed at her forehead.

Morgan shook her head, fighting for breath. Her hands moved above her head. "This just isn't going to be my day, is it?"

CHAPTER THIRTEEN

The cab circled the block for the third time. Seated in the back, Ben huddled down against the cushion. The quick-start guide for his brand-new phone covered the majority of his face. It masked his glances toward his apartment building. The driver threw him a curious look, though Ben was quick to wave him forward. When they were four blocks east of the Edgemont, Ben took his leave of the awkward-smelling vehicle, possibly infected by his own stench, and dropped a decent tip in the man's hand before departing.

He rushed back at a near run. His filthy sneakers squeaked on the wet sidewalk. Ben moved off the main road for the alley a block south. He was suddenly grateful for the change of clothes he'd purchased during his shopping excursion. There was only so long he could wear a shirt promoting Miami, having been a native Buffalonian. In truth, he needed more than a t-shirt to combat the winter cold. The wool coat helped. A new pair of pants and a navy-blue shirt completed the business casual outfit, although it did little to combat the pungent odor that had trailed him ever since the sewers.

Above, the sun was in decline. The wind took control for the coming night. It cut into him, slowing his run. Halfway into the block of back doors and emergency exits, Ben located the necessary one and headed inside.

The cafe kitchen was vacant, not that the frantic agent actually took the time to scope out the inside. After removing his new cellular device, Ben tossed the packaging. The kitchen shifted behind him as his quick steps propelled him through the shop. When he hit the dining area he stopped. Several people were seated in the place, though most appeared unaware of his entrance.

Satisfied by the casual clientele occupying the space, Ben jumped the counter, then paused to greet the only employee. The old man working the register threw him a confused stare and was met with a wave and a nod. He hated playing on the owner's somewhat faulty memory, but he had little choice in the matter.

Ben took a seat with a direct view of the large picture window lining the front of the coffee shop, but he was still deep enough into the space to avoid a random look in his direction. Before Ben could ask, the proprietor—a seventy-two-year-old widower named Hank—placed a raspberry-mango smoothie on the table. Ben thanked the gentleman, handing him a five-dollar bill in exchange for what he referred to as his Thursday usual. Faulty memory or not, Hank knew exactly what his regulars enjoyed. Ben liked that notion and the comfort that came from it, especially with what was occurring across the street.

Two men paced the block, one casually while the other played the part of a late-afternoon jogger. Another remained stationary at the front entrance. The shadow of a fourth loomed within the building, and another was in the small alley to the left of the complex. A surveillance detail at his home. He recognized three of them from the group that had tailed him during his own jogging days to the mall uptown.

Sullivan's men.

Ben muttered between fruity sips of his smoothie. "What are the chances they're looking for someone else?"

If this was Sullivan's doing, then that meant it was part of his move against Metcalf. He dialed her number, hoping for as much information as possible. Then he paused and ended the call before it connected. If they were monitoring him, then they might have been doing the same with the others. This was what Metcalf had warned him about, what she had prepared for when they spoke in Buffalo.

He simply wanted more for you. For you to do more. To be more. Those were the words shared by Metcalf while they had stood in the barren home of his former partner, Emily Wright. His father's words. They had jingled around his head, replaying on an endless loop along with the myriad questions that came with them.

Do what, exactly? Be who? Was there a simple answer, some vision his father carried for so long, as to who his son was meant to be to the world? Was he meant to be something greater than the cop he'd tried to be?

Ben held tight to the phone, remembering everything he had asked Metcalf—the promise she had made. It was his turn to keep one. To do more. To be more. He had to, for the sake of Morgan and the others—even with the consequences it brought.

The phone rang loudly, clicking over after the second ring. "Sullivan here."

Ben took a deep breath. "Yes, I'm calling about your current credit card services. Am I speaking to Grigori Soolivin?"

"Riley," Sullivan grumbled through the line. "Your plane landed hours ago. Why aren't you back for a debriefing?"

"Been busy," Ben said with a grin. "Looks like you have as well."

"Come in, Ben," Sullivan said, the threat tucked beneath the order. "It's time to make a choice."

"Already made one." The words were sharp, causing a few heads to turn in his direction. The looks did nothing to detract him.

"I was hoping you were smart enough not to fall for Susan's lies."

"No, you were hoping I wouldn't be smart enough to push for the truth. From either side. This isn't going to go the way you're hoping, Greg."

"I beg to differ," Sullivan said, an air of superiority in his voice. It was all Ben could do not to retch through the line. "I hold all the cards. Like your partner, for instance—"

"Leave Morgan out of it," Ben said, anger creeping into his voice. "Don't you—"

"I have done nothing, Ben. If you don't come in, though... well, let's just say things might happen."

"Sullivan," Ben said. "Leave her out of it."

"I'm afraid I can't do that, Riley," Sullivan said.

"You don't hold *all* the cards, Sullivan. In fact, you're missing a pretty damn big one, aren't you?"

"I don't know what you're talking about."

"The Wellspring, Greg. I know where it is."

"I… Is that right?" Sullivan asked.

"I do," Ben answered. "You can have the information. You can have it all, me included. Just leave everyone else out of it."

"Now you listen to me, Riley—"

"No thanks, Greg," Ben interrupted. He leaned forward, the speaker practically in his mouth. "Your voice honestly sounds like nails on a chalkboard to me. You want your precious Wellspring? Come and get me, Sully."

Ben snapped the phone in half, then dropped it to the floor. He stood, stomping on the device until it shattered into multiple pieces. The call had been necessary. He had baited the hook and accomplished the favor owed to Metcalf. His hope had been to divert Sullivan's full attention from the others. Ben worried his ploy hadn't been enough to satisfy the man's curiosity.

Sullivan appeared to have more pieces on the board than any of them realized. How many and how far-reaching were only two of the questions Ben raised after retrieving the shattered phone components. He tossed them into the nearby trash receptacle. For all he knew Metcalf and Morgan had already been taken. There was also the rest of the DSA to consider: Zac, the research team, security personnel, and more. He needed intel and there was only one way to get it.

He simply wanted more for you. For you to be more. To do more.

Ben sighed. He wondered about the reaction his call had caused. Across the street the surveillance team glanced around to each other, the man wrapped in shadow within the confines of the building reaching for his ear. Sullivan was contacting them. Ben hoped that meant he was wary of letting any trigger-happy agents take their shot before an attempt had been made to ask some pointed questions. For that, he was thankful. Thankful for the extra time it might offer him. It also made him hopeful that his luck might last a little longer. Sipping patiently on his smoothie, Ben monitored the team of agents surveilling the block. Incremental movements. Check-in times. After two hours, he nailed down the details: ten minutes between updates, an hour between rotations—except for the shadow within the lobby of the building, who remained unmoving throughout.

With the sun only a memory and the clouds mounting a comeback overhead, Ben slipped out the back of the shop. From there, Ben circled a wide arc around the area, hoping to avoid being picked up by a car he may have failed to track while within the confines of the shop. Two blocks over, he cut north to the rear of the complex. Within minutes he found the small fenced-in maintenance entrance. He hopped the metal mesh in a bound and landed silently along the cool concrete.

The man monitoring the alley continued to pace for the front of the building. He kicked at the debris scattered through the alley, clearly irritated with his assignment or at the hours spent in the cold. Ben sidled into a small door frame leading into the back stairwell of the building and waited.

Minutes passed. Sweat pooled around Ben's brow, but he fought the urge to swipe at it knowing it would quickly be replaced. As the man came back, Ben crept to the edge of the small shadowy alcove. The man walked without looking, tired and careless from the long day. When the short brute passed the alcove, Ben held his breath. He only needed a second.

Keep walking… keep walking…

The agent's steps shifted deeper into the darkening alleyway. Ben matched his gait and followed him closely. He brought his hands out, waiting for the right time. When he was within two feet of the agent, Ben lunged out. He wrapped an arm around the man's neck and jerked him farther into the alley and out of sight.

Ben pressed tight against the flailing agent, cutting off his air. He whispered, "Hey, tall, dark, and less than handsome. I'd rather not bust up what's left of the looks, so how about some answers?"

The struggling stopped, and Ben let his grip on the man's windpipe lessen. The agent knocked the arm away completely. "He's over—"

The arm collapsed against the man's windpipe once more. Harder. With his left fist, Ben shot out for the man's kidneys, connecting soundly. The agent fell to his knees. Ben kept the pressure up. The man reached for his sidearm. Ben slapped the weapon away and it skidded across the alley.

"Not nice," he said. "I was trying my best. Want to give it another whirl?"

"Go… to hell," the man said through desperate breaths allowed by Ben's grasp.

"How original," Ben said. The stout agent struggled harder,

and he received another gut shot as a thanks. The man dropped, straining to catch his breath. Ben retrieved the pistol on the ground. Ben loomed over him, gun in hand and leveled on the man. Ben reached for the inside pocket of the man's leather coat. "Maybe I'll skip the questions. You might not like where we head next if you play it that way, though. Understand?"

The man nodded. Ben grinned, satisfied with the thin look of hate on his captive's face. He pulled loose the badge within the coat pocket, then flipped it open.

Victor J. Newton
Security Division
Department of Special Assignments

"DSA?" Ben stood, brow furrowed. "Where did you get this?" Victor shook his head, refusing to answer. Ben pointed the gun closer. "Where's Morgan Dunleavy? Where's Metcalf?"

"Metcalf?" Victor laughed. "Good one. She went first."

"Went?" Ben choked the question out. "Where?"

The brute ran his hand along his chin, no longer fearing the weapon pointed at him. He smirked. "Not very far, from what I've heard."

Ben grabbed Victor's collar and pulled him back to his feet. He pressed the gun tight along his temple. "Answers. Now."

"I don't talk to traitors," Victor replied. "As a rule."

Traitors? Sullivan's move had been bigger than Ben had imagined. "Wow," Ben muttered. "Traitors."

"That's right."

"And you just fell in line with that story?"

It happened in an instant. The look of total satisfaction grew on Victor's face, and his gaze was no longer fixed on the questioning agent. He peered past him. Ben spun to greet the newcomer and was met with a balled-up fist to his left cheek. The blow drove him across the alley.

He fought to maintain his hold on Victor's pistol. As he steadied himself, another punch landed below Ben's ribs and drove him off his feet. He slammed into the wall of his apartment building, where he slid along the brick exterior to the alley floor. The gun slipped from his hand, and a recently shined black shoe kicked it farther away. Ben's vision failed him, blocked by blood pouring from his brow. When it returned, he was staring down the thick barrel of a gun.

"Of course he did, Riley. He's a good agent. You could learn a thing or two from him."

Ben recognized the voice in an instant. Deep and gravelly, like a walking, talking concrete mixer. Spots faded from his view and the alley returned. So did the man's face. Scars covered his left side, and the eye was twice the size of its companion. His lips ran in a sneer along the right. The man's left side was no longer functional from the scabbed-over burns running down the length of his face and neck.

After Chicago, when the FBI had only recovered three burned bodies in the wreckage of the abandoned hospital, Ben had known. Without a doubt, there was no question who survived the blast. He had simply hoped to never see the monster again.

Connor Hendricks.

CHAPTER FOURTEEN

Sullivan slammed the phone against the desk. He squeezed the thin plastic case beneath his fingers. A low growl of disdain grew from his lips. The device slid along the surface until it crashed into a framed photo of him with the president.

That had been a lifetime ago. The man had placated and handled Sullivan as he had with all the new congressional recruits only to stab them in the back when the chips were down. It was a lesson Sullivan had carried with him ever since.

Riley was playing for time. That was his first thought after the call. The cornered agent had recognized the long odds of the day ahead of him and was bargaining for his life by using the one tool left in his arsenal.

The Wellspring.

Yet, did he know the truth behind it? Could Riley actually know its location? When the enigmatic instrument had gone missing Sullivan had assumed outside forces were involved. Metcalf had come to mind immediately, especially considering her disappearing act so soon after the call. His intel suggested other possibilities. Had Riley known all along? Was that why he had been at that house on Wex that night in Buffalo? Had he been working with Metcalf longer than Sullivan imagined?

Damn the man. And damn me for believing a word out of his mouth.

The chance existed, and as long as it remained, Sullivan could do little. He snatched the walkie talkie from its standing position on the far side of his desk. Static crackled through the line, so he thumbed the control until it went silent.

"I need Riley brought in alive," his voice commanded. "Divert all available personnel to finding him."

He placed the radio down and closed his eyes. Focus on one allowed the others more opportunities for escape. Was that the ploy? Clever for a runt like Riley. The subtle manipulation sounded more like Metcalf, but it couldn't possibly be her. Not after her tragic accident.

A wry grin spread from the corner of his lip. The radio returned to his hand. "Kill the others."

It was time to make an end of things. Any lingering doubt of his intentions no longer entered his thoughts. His moves were too public. Failure was an unthinkable outcome in his view.

Sullivan settled against his chair. Metcalf's office served him well, though the space remained locked in the dungeon-like aesthetic of the rest of the warehouse. Before he was able to relax along the cushion of the chair, his phone rang. He reached out to grab the device cradled along the base of the lone photo on display, then sighed. He accepted the call nonetheless.

"What is it?"

"Greg?" Stallworth asked, agitation in his voice.

Sullivan bit his lip, recalling his place in the chain of command. It was another change long past due. For the moment, he swallowed his ambition. "Apologies, Donald. A long day."

"One well worth it, I hope. Considering the stakes."

Removing Metcalf was not the issue. The Council backed the plan and had for weeks, thanks to his slowly revealed misgivings and the mounting evidence that had accumulated. Subtle hints at the benefit of her dismissal had played better than a power grab.

However, with Metcalf dead, his safety net had vanished and his true priority now stood revealed. He needed the Wellspring in hand. Without it, he had earned nothing but a swift response from the Trust. They were a group bent on living in the past instead of seizing the future.

Without the Wellspring, all would be for naught. Stallworth failed to look past such things, especially when it infringed on his lifestyle choices.

"What can I do for you?" Sullivan asked, feigning interest.

"The Council wants to meet."

"Delay them. I'm busy."

"They have concerns over what happened this morning,"

Stallworth continued. "The accident with Susan and how it looks from their —"

"I'm aware of the optics. I also care little for their view of things. I had nothing to do with what happened, and neither did you. Any investigation into the matter will make that clear. Instead of focusing on it, we should use this time with Susan out of the way to —"

"Stop," Stallworth ordered. "Dammit, Greg. We have no one to blame if anything goes wrong. The accident is playing on the news and shining a light on our affairs. We *can't* afford another mistake. If the Trust finds out what we've planned —"

"They won't," Sullivan reassured the man. He lowered his voice at the sight of a shadow along the door. Zac stood in the frame. The newly installed director of the department waved him inside the office. "Stall them, Donald. I have everything well in hand."

"But —"

Sullivan ended the call and turned off the device. Then, he silenced the walkie talkie at his side. His smile returned as he greeted his visitor. It was his public face over the growing concern mounting in the background.

"I could use some good news, Zac."

Zac took the seat across from him. Sullivan settled in his own, hands clasped in front of him.

"The files are almost unlocked, sir," Zac started. He dabbed at the thin line of sweat along his brow. "Should only be a matter of hours."

"See that it is, Zac."

"Anything wrong, sir?"

Sullivan paused, checking his tone before speaking. "Minor annoyances. Nothing more. The important thing is the whereabouts of the Wellspring."

"The files might bring us nothing."

"I'm aware. Which is why, after their interview with the Security Division, the rest of the staff will be shifting to that priority as well."

"No one had anything to do with the director's — I mean, Metcalf's — decisions," Zac said.

"I know, Zac. But with something as sensitive as this? The Wellspring is too important."

"What is it exactly?"

Sullivan stood, then started pacing around the desk. "The future, Zac. The Wellspring is the future of the human race." He stopped and shook his head. "Sorry. I tend to settle into melodramatics on occasion."

He rested a hand on the arm of the chair. "In the last fifty years mankind has progressed faster and farther than they have in the previous 4,000. Why do you think that is?"

"Technology," Zac answered. "Science? Our ingenuity as a species has—"

"Been helped along."

Zac's eyes widened. "What?"

"In 1968, when three brilliant men sat around the table and discovered a way for a small microchip to house millions of bits of data, it wasn't by chance."

"Are you saying—?"

Sullivan raised a hand. "When Otto Hahn first discovered fission, a process that eventually resulted in the atomic explosion that ended the Second World War, it was not without assistance."

"The Wellspring?"

"It has put us on a path. I, for one, would like to see where it goes. Wouldn't you?"

"Sir, what you're saying… If such a thing was possible—"

"Find it, Zac," Sullivan said. He stood and moved for the door. He needed Zac motivated; he needed him curious. With questions in hand, the answers would come faster. Sullivan was counting on that from Zac. "Together we can shape the future of the country—of the world. I need you to find it, Zac. It has to be quickly, though, or everything we've fought for here today will be lost."

CHAPTER FIFTEEN

"Do not move!" the lead agent barked. "Keep those hands up."

"This is a mistake, guys," Morgan said through gritted teeth. Grissom's backup team kept her locked down on her knees. All five trigger-happy agents tightened the noose with each step they took. Time was against her and she needed an opening—any opening. "I'm DSA. Same as you it seems. My badge number is—"

"Suspended pending inquiry," the agent said. "We know who you were, Agent Dunleavy."

Cold stares caught her from the other members of the team. They didn't want an argument. They wanted this clean. The two men to the rear of the half circle tried to block the concerned citizens nearby from the drama unfolding in the lobby of the apartment complex. Dozens of eyes landed on her, but she refused to reciprocate, staying with the agent in charge as much as possible.

Out of the departing crowd, a lone figure stood in the corner. Obscured by a thick coat and a wide-brimmed hat, they refused to follow the rest in their flight from the lobby. There was something in the stance of the figure, and the way they remained in the shadows of the room even with the bright lights overhead.

"I'd like to talk to Metcalf," Morgan declared.

"I'm sure you would," another agent said with a chuckle. He jabbed an elbow into his colleague to the right and the pair shared a laugh. "Traitors stick together, don't they?"

The lead agent, whom she silently referred to as *Agent One*, threw the jovial subordinate a thin glare. The laughter faded in an instant. He crouched in front of her. "Susan Metcalf was killed en route to holding early this morning. Car accident."

"What did you just say?" Morgan's hands fell, the shock of his statement causing her to forget about her current predicament. *Metcalf's dead? What the hell was going on?*

Agent One jumped back from her sudden shift, and the others leveled their sidearms on her. "I said don't—"

"I'm not moving!" Morgan yelled, rubbing her eyes. "I'm not…"

From the corner of the lobby the lone figure bolted for her position. The large hat and over-sized coat peeled away to reveal a lithe figure Morgan recognized immediately. Stephanie Atwater moved toward the two men in the rear in a single stride with fists clenched tight at her sides.

Morgan's smile caught Agent One by surprise. "But *you* should."

The agents shifted at once. The confidence behind her words startled them. By the time they reprioritized their focus it was too late. The woman was within arm's reach of the two agents. She grabbed the barrels of their weapons and yanked both men toward her. Off balance, they stumbled forward a step. The one on the right was greeted by a firm kick to the ribs. The woman's right fist shot out and clipped the second faltering oaf in the temple hard. Without missing a beat, Morgan's liberator moved into the middle of the crowd of agents, refusing to let them bring their high-caliber overcompensation into play. The first two slowly recovered from her assault while she met with her third playmate. Morgan jumped to her feet, eager to join in the fun.

Agent One, diverted by the blond's attack, failed to notice Morgan's approach. Morgan tapped his shoulder twice, letting her hand rest on it the third time. She spun him around with her left hand and her right shot out directly at his nose. His eyes rolled back, but her fist connected twice more before she let his bloodied body fall to the carpet.

She moved for another agent, who frantically searched for a better position. He raised his gun against her and Morgan realized the distance was too great to cover. She watched him take aim, then rolled left when he spun right. Bullets sailed wide from the automatic weapon. Taking advantage of his disorientation, Morgan's leg swung out, caught him at the knees, and knocked him to the ground. She collapsed on him in an instant, forcing the air from his lungs. She pulled the gun loose and tossed it aside. Then she felt his nose crunch from her assault. He collapsed against the carpet, unconscious.

Breathing hard, Morgan moved to handle anyone else standing. Luckily, the blond had things well in hand. She danced between her first two victims — her third was curled up in a ball on the far side of the lobby. Confidence in each movement, she ducked and dodged around their pitiful attempts to contain her. Morgan could only play the role of spectator while her savior led the last two men merrily around the lobby. The first went down in seconds from a shot to his throat. He choked for air when her leg came down, and the decisive blow shattered his ankle. The second, who appeared to be better trained, slipped up in his haste and telegraphed his strike. She caught his sloppy blow and tossed him toward Morgan. He was met with a tooth-filled grin and a hard punch across his cheek, which sent him to the floor.

Silence greeted them.

Both women caught their breath, prepared for another round. The team of agents remained on the floor, unable or unwilling to continue. Morgan held tight to her hips as she grinned in awe at her rescuer.

"Ready to go?" Stephanie Atwater asked.

"How the hell did you do that?"

Stephanie laughed at her confusion. "Did you think I was just a pretty face at the office?"

"Honestly? Yeah." For as long as she had worked with the short blond, Morgan thought of her as a glorified secretary to Metcalf. Mostly because that was, in fact, her role in the office.

The two collected the firearms scattered across the floor. Morgan tucked two pistols into the waistband of her sweatpants. Stephanie tossed the rest in a nearby receptacle. As they made their way to the exit, both peered back. The men were beginning to stir.

"We need to move," Stephanie said.

"Tell him that," Morgan replied, pointing to the towering figure at the base of the stairwell.

Stephanie's face dropped, unable to move for a moment. "Agent Grissom?"

"Not anymore, Stephanie. We need to..." Stephanie was frozen in place. Morgan pointed at the raised hands of the former field team leader. There was a weapon in each of them. His dead eyes beamed brighter than the overhead lights. Morgan pulled at her companion. "Move it, Stephanie! Move it!"

Gunfire rang out. The glass door shattered before them. They leapt through the broken mess for the sidewalk beyond. Cold shot up Morgan's legs as her naked feet stumbled through the melting snow gathered along the walkway. In her haste to escape, Stephanie was unable to make the initial turn and slammed into a parked van. Morgan grabbed her hand and dragged her to her feet before the pair raced down the block. They stayed low, more shots ringing out and cutting a swath through the front edifice of the building.

They dove clear and kept their heads tucked low until only the sound of sirens in the distance filled the air. Stephanie led the way while Morgan cursed the cold raging through her body.

"Thanks back there. I don't—"

"Thank me later," Morgan said. Her naked feet screamed with each step.

"Right," Stephanie said. "Come on, we need to—"

"Wait." Morgan held up the fleeing blond. They huddled against the corner of the building, ducking against the shadows of the alley.

The five agents staggered from the building and started for the parked van waiting for them. None glanced in their direction. They made no movement to pursue. Instead, the van's engine roared to life and the screech of tires sent the agents in the opposite direction.

"Where the hell are they going?"

Stephanie tugged at the woman's bare shoulder. "They must have bigger fish to fry. We, on the other hand, have our own concerns at the moment."

Grissom arrived at the sidewalk. There was no distracting his cause. His eyes had shifted back to a blazing blue. They locked on target, trailing them from the corner of the building. The pair rushed into oncoming traffic, ducking between cars as horns boomed through the streets of Bethesda.

"Run, Morgan!"

She did, with everything left in her. She ran, despite the cold giving her chills inside and out. Despite the confession from the man who had recruited her—who had saved her. Despite the terror at realizing her entire career with the DSA had been nothing but a lie.

She ran, hoping for the chance to make sense of things. She prayed for a chance to make it right.

CHAPTER SIXTEEN

"I can't believe the luck of it all."

Luck. That was not the word Ben would have chosen to describe his current situation. Connor Hendricks was a mercenary psychopath bent on murdering anyone that stood in the way of his objectives. Ben had ended up being one of those people. Luck was how he described their one and only encounter when Hendricks — his true name an unsolved mystery — had been caught in the path of a pyrokinetic named Henry Reed and been flash fried with the rest of his wetwork team in an abandoned hospital.

Only he hadn't been. He had survived, horribly scarred down his left side.

Yeah, Ben thought. *Lucky me.*

Victor kept Ben's arms locked behind his back. Hendricks' fist slammed against Ben's left cheek. Skin ripped away from the blow. Blood filled his mouth.

"Here I am, quite the independent contractor — doing my part for my country, of course — and who just happens to call me? Now, I know what you're thinking. Did I really want to become a simple employee rather than be my own man with my own team and ambitions? Well, Riley, a man has to eat, doesn't he?"

Ben spat a thick wad of blood, and immediately felt its replacement running along his bottom lip. "Let me guess. Big veal diet?"

Hendricks' fist shot out again, delivering a punch to the gut this time. Victor hooked under Ben's arms. He refused to let Ben fall. Hendricks grabbed a mop of hair and pulled Ben's head up.

"Keep talking, Riley. This is the most fun I've had in months." He wiped the blood from his knuckles with pride.

"Now where was I? Oh, yeah. I get the call for pyro boy. He made quite the mess and someone had to clean it up. Remember that?"

"I remember the hospital exploding," Ben said, his struggle for release ending with a groan. His left cheek had swelled up to the point of blocking part of his vision.

Ben's concern turned to the story being told — about the people who had hired Hendricks, who had created the Promethean drug in the first place. Somehow it tied everything together: every event since his arrival at the DSA. He grinned at the mercenary. "I only wish I could have seen the look on your face. Probably can't show it to me anymore, can you, Hendricks?"

His left eye went dark as another right cross connected with the pulpy flesh. Heat ran down his face alongside the growing stream of blood. It was mostly his own, with a little of Hendricks' mixed in for good measure.

"You killed my men," Hendricks snapped, leaning in close. "I wasn't real attached to them; it's just the point of the matter. Professional courtesy and all that crap."

Ben's smile widened. "Didn't you get my sympathy card? It had a kitty hanging from a tree saying I don't give a flying —"

The force of Hendricks' strike drove Ben down to the concrete. Victor let the agent drop this time and backed away from the conflict.

The disgusted member of the security team pulled at the vindictive Hendricks. "We should probably —"

"Shut it," Hendricks replied without looking. He loomed over the crawling agent. "You know the kicker, Riley? I come to find — after a grueling rehab, by the way — that you simply handed the kid over to the same guy who hired me."

"What?"

"Sullivan had meant to take Kane out quietly and the boy screwed the pooch," Hendricks said. "Too loud. Too public. So he sent me in to clean up the mess before too many eyes turned their attention to his dealings."

"No."

Ben stopped. The truth hurt worse than any of the punches by the cold-blooded killer. *Sullivan?* Sullivan had been behind Chicago? How? How far did his connections carry him? Sullivan's power play for the DSA was bigger than a single department. He served outside interests; someone else pulled his strings. There was something bigger occurring, and it was much more far reaching than any of them had guessed.

"Yes, Riley, that's right," Hendricks laughed. "I lost an entire team for no reason. All I had to do was let you and Henry just walk the entire time. My objective was completed either way."

"You're wrong. Henry is—"

"Wake up, Riley." Hendricks jabbed his foot into Ben's back and held him against the pavement. "I mean, kudos for the dedication to your job. And thanks for that look on your face, by the way. Almost makes the whole thing worth it."

"You're lying," Ben muttered, running through everything in his mind. They had extracted Henry from Chicago. They had relocated him to one of their private facilities. "Henry's safe. He's protected."

"By the DSA," Hendricks said, pointing to the logo on his blue flak jacket. "The so-called Department of Special Assignments. They won't even tell you its real purpose. You still have no idea what the DSA is, do you? Do you even know who you've really been working for this whole time?"

Hendricks kicked Ben in the ribs. His laughter roared, concealing the footfalls of the rest of his team gathering in the alley. Looks of contentment at a job well done shot between them. They slapped hands with excitement. Their joy faded, however, the second Hendricks removed his sidearm and held it to Ben's head.

"The Trust has manipulated your little department since the beginning, Riley," Hendricks said with a smirk. "Every operation. Every objective. They've had a hand in it all. Some indirectly, thanks to the Council. Others directly, thanks to people like Sullivan and Grissom."

"Grissom?"

"You didn't know, did you?" Laughter lifted the man up just as he brought another blow down upon his captive. "I'll leave you to mull all that over."

"What are you doing?" Victor asked, reaching for the gun.

Hendricks pulled away, his sidearm never straying from the target. "Taking out a piece of treasonous trash. Problem with that?"

The others shook their heads. Victor slapped them down with

a look, then moved to cut Hendricks off from his target. "You heard the update from base. This ass is to be brought in alive. He has vital information for the director about the location of the Wellspring. Kill orders for the rest."

"Morgan…" Ben uttered, fighting to get to his knees. He had hoped to buy her more time with his bluff; he had hoped to save her from the pain coursing through his body. Now he could only hope she was fast enough to escape Sullivan's reach.

"We're taking him in," Victor continued. "Sullivan's orders."

Hendricks nodded slowly, lowering his sidearm. "You're right, Agent. My mistake."

Victor turned to coordinate with the rest of the squad. It was the last thing he ever did. Hendricks' weapon rose quickly. The sound of a single shot swallowed all sound in the alley. Victor dropped like a stone. As he fell, the three other members of the surveillance team grabbed for their weapons.

Hendricks was too far ahead of them to be stopped. One bullet each at close range ended the debate over Ben's fate before another word could be muttered. Each man was dead before they hit the ground. Lifeless husks filled the alley around the bleeding Ben Riley.

"Well," Hendricks said with a sneer. "More like your mistake."

"Hendricks!" Ben screamed, blood spraying from his lips. He fought to balance on his knees. "You son of a bitch!"

"Stop with the pet names, Riley."

Ben looked at the four dead men surrounding him like the arrows on a compass. They were nothing more than collateral damage to the soulless mercenary. "Why, Hendricks?"

Hendricks huffed, pulling Ben to his feet. He drove Ben back against the cold brick of the apartment building. "You think I give a damn about Sullivan's power grab? About the Wellspring? I took this job for one reason. You."

Ben stared down the barrel of the psycho's gun. "I'll kill you for this."

Hendricks' hand wrapped tight around the bleeding agent's throat as he whispered in Ben's ear. "You'll try."

CHAPTER SEVENTEEN

Zac ran his fingers across his eyes, rubbing away the weariness without success. The long day continued, hours of searching through locked databases and terminal logs for information. He had lost hours deep in thought. Half had been on the task ahead and the other, more pertinent half, had been locked on the past.

It was those damn suitcases in his trunk. When he left his desk, coffee cup in hand and caffeine fix long past due, he took the long way to the break room so he could stop at the fourth-floor domiciles. There were plenty of open rooms available. Half of the staff had been dismissed following their interviews — some by request, others less politely. No arrests had been made, thankfully.

After selecting a room, a temporary solution to his housing crisis, Zac returned to the first floor and the waiting break room. The coffee steamed to the lip of the cup, soothing and relaxing; it was a momentary pause from the storm swirling in his head.

Only the work remained, which was taking far longer than he had imagined. The encryption he had installed on Metcalf's data months earlier went quickly. A simple recoding and passkey allowed him to slip in the back door. Unfortunately, Metcalf had gone one step further. The code work appeared recent, blocking his access to the secret files. Zac recognized the user behind it immediately.

A plant in his operation to monitor him, Adler was the reason so much information of late had skirted around his office. She was why things had circumvented his authority with ease. Hell, he had even assisted in screwing himself over, since his personal problems had clouded his judgment to the point of passing off priorities. Adler served Metcalf's agenda and no one else.

Who did *he* serve?

Sullivan had offered him a chance to continue the work, to make amends for the mistakes of the past. The man's obsession with the Wellspring bordered on extreme, however. And his discussions with their NSA liaison on the Inter-Agency Council had become increasingly heated. There was more going on in the background. Promises had been made to be more open, to move past the trust issues that plagued Metcalf's time in charge. It was all meant to end with her dismissal.

With her death.

He had read the after-action report from one of the survivors of the crash. Martin was the agent's name. He described the collision, but little of what happened after. He had barely cleared the wreckage before the van had gone up in flames. Metcalf's burnt body was taken to the morgue for identification through dental records kept on file.

It came back positive.

She had been killed on impact. Her arrest had turned out to be her final sentencing. Zac found himself locked on that moment during his hunt for the truth—his quest for the mysterious Wellspring. She had kept it hidden for a reason. It was another secret, just like Sullivan's true intentions. So many secrets, and Zac was stuck in between them all. Loyalty to an agency or a person? What was right and what was wrong?

Zac powered into the restroom at the end of the first-floor corridor. He slammed the door open and headed for the closest sink. He slammed his coffee cup on the narrow ledge. It teetered then tipped into the sink. Coffee spilled all over the porcelain base. It was quickly joined by the contents of Zac's stomach. He heaved hard, nerves rattling down his intestines and back up again. When he finished, he lifted the cup from the sink and tossed it in the garbage.

When he returned to the sink, and the mirror hanging in front of him, Zac hardly recognized himself. A ghost of a man stood before him. The events of the day were ripping away at him, clawing away everything decent about his life. So many questions about his wife and Morgan, were now joined by his work debate. It had been too much for too long. The evidence was conclusive in the blank eyes of the figure in the mirror.

He had found the location of the Wellspring. His next decision would either set Sullivan on his quest or damn the agency he'd served proudly for years. He didn't know what to do; he honestly didn't know how to do anything anymore. If he failed to offer the truth to the director he put his family at risk. He had grown tired of putting Claire and Alex in the firing line for his mistakes. They were all that mattered. More than Morgan and the excitement that came with her. More than his work and the fulfillment at helping solve complicated cases around the country. He had screwed up and hurt Claire more than words could ever express or apologies could ever heal, no matter the time lapsed.

He owed her better. He needed to make good on that promise. No one else would. He had to keep them safe, no matter the cost. No matter the truth behind the DSA, behind Sullivan, and behind the Wellspring.

"Do the work, Zac," he muttered to the mystery man in the mirror. "Tell him the truth, and then go home."

It was a simple plan. The best kind.

His plan immediately disappeared when the stall door behind him opened. His eyes widened and his jaw fell open at the figure waiting within the men's room the entire time. A duffel bag rested on the toilet behind the man, and another was strapped over his shoulder. He held tight to a pistol aimed directly at Zac.

Lincoln grinned. "Good to see you too, Modine. Real good."

CHAPTER EIGHTEEN

Her feet went numb. She knew they were still attached as she continued her flight deeper into the web of downtown Bethesda. The meaty pieces of flesh slapped pavement but, for Morgan, they no longer held any feeling whatsoever. She worried that the sensation would continue to fade up her legs until it over-whelmed her completely.

Stephanie failed to perceive Morgan's terror. She pulled at the chilled agent, guiding her around stopped cars and through oncoming traffic. The din of horns, the flashing of lights, and the screams of the evening commute filled their ears, especially con-sidering most of the sounds were directed toward them. Cars barely missed them, a number of them came dangerously close, yet the personal assistant—somehow turned blond badass—ignored the risk in their hunt for an escape route.

Morgan followed to the best of her abilities. She feared the end. More than that, she feared living with what she now knew to be true. She had fought against it for so long, the truth behind the DSA. The lies and the betrayal, the agendas in the back-ground, all that she had ignored for so long was now blatantly displayed in each passing thought. Grissom had lied. Everything behind his intentions had served his own ends. His true loyalties had caused his death. Not Metcalf, not the mission, but Gris-som's allegiance to a shadow organization called the Trust.

It burned at her and slowed her pace. Stephanie continued on, reaching back to prod the spiraling agent along. Hope rested in Stephanie's eyes. Morgan no longer held any. Still, they fled through the winding traffic.

"Any idea where we're going?" Morgan called.

Stephanie turned right, narrowly avoiding a collision with a semi making a wide turn. They left the main thread of traffic for a connecting secondary street. "Yes."

"Okay," Morgan said, drawing out the word. "Care to share it?"

No reply came. Stephanie merely continued their running tour of the city. More concerns took root for Morgan, especially the lack of contact with Ben. If agents had been waiting for her, there stood a more-than-reasonable chance he was on their target list as well. With no phone it was impossible to warn him.

At least she had some protection now. Both pistols were tucked along the small of her back and both were loaded. They meant little in deterring the machine once known as Jacob Grissom, but they brought her a small measure of comfort.

Stephanie paused at the end of the block, hair whipping in the wind. She peered back and grimaced. "He's closing too quickly."

He was only a block behind them. Grissom's pace never allowed them to slip out of sight for even a second. The chase was the endgame for him. "I'm open to suggestions."

"Come on," Stephanie snapped. She pointed ahead at a lone figure on the sidewalk. The young man juggled his keys, a briefcase, and a bag of groceries. Stephanie bumped into him hard, and the keys flew loose to her waiting hand. The truck, well-maintained and sparkling despite the winter weather, chimed; the doors unlocked, and the alarm deactivated.

"Hey!" the man cried. His groceries fell from his hand and scattered along the pavement. "What the hell are you doing?"

"Emergency," Stephanie said as she hopped into the driver's seat. The engine roared to life and she shrugged. "Sorry about this."

Morgan patted his shoulder before joining her in the waiting vehicle. "We're federal agents, if that helps."

"It doesn't!"

"I didn't think it would."

Morgan slammed the door and the truck veered into traffic. Horns blared, middle fingers were raised — including that of the man left with his spilt groceries. The leather seats in the car shot more cold through her than the outdoors. Stephanie, quick to notice, blasted the heat and turned the vents toward her shivering companion.

When her focus returned to the road, an SUV was double-parked in front of them. The squealing of brakes and the jerking of the wheel sent the truck swerving across the lane to avoid the collision. Morgan and Stephanie quietly settled into their seats as traffic thinned. They passed multiple intersections and distance grew with each frozen breath.

"I can't see him," Stephanie said, relieved. "I think we lost him."

Movement caught Morgan's attention. She leaned close to the passenger side mirror a second before it shattered. The entire assembly fell away as another bullet sheared it from the vehicle.

"He's still there."

Grissom barreled down the median, avoiding all traffic, his eyes aglow in red once more. His gait closed the gap despite Stephanie's foot pressing on the accelerator. He didn't have to get closer, it seemed. The broken mirror attested to his aim, which appeared to be controlled by his shifting irises and his steady arm. He *wanted* to get closer.

"How could Jake let this happen?" Morgan asked.

"What *did* happen?" Stephanie said. The truck took a sharp right, never losing momentum as it journeyed north. "He say anything?"

She hesitated, unsure how much to share. "Something about Sullivan, but that doesn't make sense."

"Actually, it makes perfect sense," Stephanie said. She continued to glance at her mirror to keep their pursuer in full view. "All this? This is all Sullivan."

"Why?"

"He's after —"

The back window cracked, and the rearview mirror became a casualty of the latest bullet. Time was running out quickly.

"Listen," Morgan said. "The last time I saw Grissom was when we infiltrated an unsanctioned lab run by a disavowed scientist. Oliver Blake had developed a number of viruses and pathogens, all incredibly deadly. Grissom was infected on site, and he died. Or we thought he died."

"The infection must have been a primer," Stephanie said. "Neutralized the subject without killing him. Then Sullivan's people took care of the rest."

"What people? Who is he working for? Stephanie, who are *we* working for right now?"

"The good guys, Morgan," she said. "Promise."

"I wish I could believe you."

The truck turned, and more bullets rushed by. "Almost there."

Downtown faded behind them. In its place was a vacant street at the city limits. Apartments sprouted up on both sides of the lane, and there was a park in the distance. Stephanie's breath slowed, calming from the pursuit. Morgan, however, felt her back tense up at the lack of answers from her colleague.

"Where? Stephanie, what are we doing here?"

"We're—" Terror filled her eyes and she fell silent.

"Steph?" Morgan asked. "What is it? What—?"

Grissom stood in the middle of the road. In front of them. For all his patience, for all his prodding throughout the merry chase through Bethesda, he hadn't seemed to grow tired, and he hadn't stopped for a second. He showed no signs of exhaustion, no fatigue of any sort. He wasn't human. Not to Morgan. Not any longer.

"Dammit, Steph, look—"

The first shot took out their front tire. The second followed in quick succession and the windshield splintered from the impact. They could no longer see anything in front of them.

"Crap," Stephanie muttered. "Hang on."

The car jerked right, fighting against her control. Another shot, and suddenly the truck was on its side. Sparks flew at Morgan, the screeching of metal on the pavement matching her screams in intensity. The vehicle skidded to a halt in the gutter.

Stephanie kicked the windshield out. Once outside, she pulled Morgan to safety. She tossed the dazed agent behind the wall created by the tipped truck before joining her. Bullets pinged against the frame, slow and steady. Each shift to one side or the other of the truck brought with it another shot, each one closer than the last. The chase was over.

They were trapped.

CHAPTER NINETEEN

Bullets met their attempts to flee. When they shifted to the rear of the truck they were met with a barrage. The same occurred when they crept toward the front. Each missed the mark, but each blocked their escape. The two women were pinned against their small patch of sidewalk. Morgan realized the intention behind the perfectly placed shots. Only Grissom would decide when to make an end of things with them.

Stephanie hunkered near the crumpled hood, hands tight over her ears. Morgan tried to make out the words slipping from her lips. The constant gunfire made the task impossible. Stephanie never repeated herself, turning her back to Morgan. It was as if she wasn't talking to Morgan at all.

Determined to play against expectation, Morgan leapt to her feet. One of the borrowed semi-automatics slipped into her waiting hand, and she unloaded it on the surprised assassin. He twisted his body, shielding his face from the assault with his arm. Shells pounded against his midsection, forcing him back a step, then two, though never enough to bring him down. The enhancements saw to that.

When the chamber clicked, Morgan dropped to her knees. Shots flew overhead; rushing air caught in their wake. They had been kill shots, to be sure. She had failed to side with him, to understand his decisions. Any further conversation was irrelevant.

"We're trapped," Stephanie called. "We're not going to make it."

Wherever Stephanie had been taking them, this wasn't it. The confidence displayed by the blond when she had taken out three highly trained operatives in the lobby of Morgan's apartment building with ease, was now replaced by concern and fear.

"Where?"

Stephanie shook her head, beating the back of her head lightly against the roof of the crashed truck. She wasn't a field agent, and she likely wasn't used to the sudden shifts that came in operations. There were always unknown variables involved and the field team had been trained to calculate them at a moment's notice.

Morgan tossed the empty pistol aside and retrieved her other weapon from her waistband. The cold metal was a comfort compared to the blisters forming along her toes. She held the piece out to Stephanie, who promptly turned it down.

Morgan cocked an eyebrow. "Don't be ridiculous."

"Me?" Stephanie said, hand over her heart. "I'm not your partner."

"Seriously? Right now with the jokes?"

Stephanie forced a nervous smile. "You'll need it."

"Why?" She didn't think any weapon would do much good having seen the effect of an entire clip wasted on Grissom. That effect being nada, zip, zero, zilch. Unfortunately, it was all she had left. It was the only tool available to buy them enough time to scatter and regroup. Stephanie, however, continued to search the block, muttering under her breath like there was another plan in place somehow.

"Listen…" Stephanie started. Morgan shook her head immediately.

"No."

Another barrage of shots connected with the building behind them. Grissom refused to walk away, refused to leave them a moment's peace. His presence filled the air just as much as the spray of seemingly never-ending bullets at his disposal.

"We don't have time to argue, Morgan. Here." The blond removed a small earpiece and held it out.

"What are you doing?"

"I'd clean it first, but… sorry. I know, another joke."

"I'm not—"

"Put it in," Stephanie demanded. Her eyes watered. She took in deep breaths, her body shaking.

"What are you doing?"

She shifted to the rear of the truck. "Giving you both a shot."

"Stephanie, don't..." Morgan tried to reach for her, but Stephanie caught her hand.

"Morgan," she said. "The DSA is just a name. The work you did, though? What you still have to do? It means something. Remember that." She pointed to the earpiece. "And trust her. Please."

"No. Don't even —"

She was gone before Morgan could react. She ran out into the street and raced down the block away from the park. Morgan froze, nothing more than a witness to the act. Then Grissom turned toward the fleeing woman.

Morgan shot up from the protection of the truck, firing blind at the mammoth in the middle of traffic. She screamed as she unloaded the full clip of the pistol on the man who had recruited her to the DSA. It didn't make a bit of difference. Most were wide, missing the mark completely. Others found Grissom but had no effect. He didn't even bother to look at her. His left arm provided cover for his head while his right took aim at Stephanie.

"Morgan," the earpiece chirped.

Morgan dropped the empty weapon. "Hello?"

"The park," the voice roared. Wind cut through the small speaker. "On your left. One hundred meters."

"But Stephanie —!" Morgan shouted.

"I'm aware. I've been monitoring the line, but I need you to run —"

Morgan stepped out from behind the truck. "Jake!"

He turned toward her, the gun still leveled down the street, still locked on her rescuer. "I offered you my hand, Morgan. This could have been avoided if only you had listened."

"No one else has to die, Jake," Morgan said. "Please."

"This isn't on me," Grissom replied, the gun never straying from the fleeing target. "This is on you."

"Don't you dare put this on me! Don't you —"

"Go!" the voice in her ear yelled. "Now!"

Morgan ran, her naked feet skidding along the wet pavement. The shot sounded a dozen steps into her escape. She glanced back, still racing for the snow-covered park in the distance. The body had fallen without a sound. Long strands of hair danced in the air as Stephanie met the cold concrete.

Morgan wanted nothing more than to go back and help her fallen friend. She wanted to believe a part of Grissom had held back and Stephanie wasn't dead.

The truth, however, was clear. There was no saving her friend, the woman who had sacrificed all for her escape. There was only the waiting park at the end of the block. Morgan focused every bit of willpower, propelling herself farther and faster toward the snow.

"Now what?" she asked, her heart pounding in her ears.

"Run like hell."

Morgan searched the park ahead as she cleared the entrance. There was no cover. There were no trees until the far side. There was nothing but open air and lots of snow.

"Some plan."

"Do it," the voice commanded. Grissom's heavy footfalls thundered behind her. There was no more toying with his prey. His hunt was over.

She pushed harder and prayed her bare feet wouldn't slip in the snow. All Grissom needed was one decent shot and it was over. One second to aim, one more to pull the trigger, and it ended. Just like Stephanie, dead thanks to Morgan's inability to do the same to the man stalking them.

"He's coming," the fleeing agent said. "Now would be a good time for some kind of plan."

The voice was gone. Only the sound of her heart pounding remained. Her breath wheezed in the cold night air. The numb feeling settled in her feet and up her legs. *Any second now*, she thought. *Any second Grissom is going to fire and…*

"Morgan," the voice ended her dizzying thoughts. "Get down."

She dropped. The bullet whizzed overhead. Sliding across the snow, Morgan hit the ground with a solid thud. She rolled over onto her stomach for a glance behind her. Bitter cold pulsed through her clothes. Her feet no longer registered on any level. Her body was failing her at the worst possible moment.

Grissom caught up. His shadow stretched across her broken and bruised frame. His jaw clicked loudly, gears grinding with each motion. "Morgan."

"Stay down," the voice said calmly in her ear.

"You killed her," Morgan snapped through her terror.

"You made your choice," Grissom said, finger on the trigger. "I made mine."

Morgan closed her eyes. It was better this way; it was better to let it end. Everything was gone. Her job. Her friends—not that there ever were more than a handful of people that fell into that category. She believed she'd earned the second chance offered her when she had joined the DSA. She had thought she was working to make the country—if not the world—a better place. It was all lies. All smoke and mirrors in a game she had never wanted to play.

Nevertheless, it was her life, faults and all. And damn anyone that tried to take it from her. Even Grissom. Her eyes opened, and her body rose to meet the waiting pistol in the mammoth's hand. She refused to lie down, refused to allow everything to end without a fight.

To the south of the park behind Grissom were a number of apartment buildings. On the rooftop of one a soft flash of light reflected from the moonlight.

A rifle scope.

"Headshot!" Morgan screamed into the earpiece. "Make it a...!"

The sound of the shot echoed in the field. Grissom stood still for a long moment, still poised to fire. Blue eyes sparked bright with awareness.

"Morg—"

Grissom fell. Blood spurted from the open wound at the side of his skull and his body crashed to the earth. His gun dropped into the nearby snow. She reached for it instinctively. Once she found her feet, Morgan steadied the weapon on the unmoving figure sprawled in the snow. Any sign of the light in Grissom's eyes faded.

Slowly, Morgan faced the high-rise in the distance. The reflected light off the scope was gone, replaced by the standing silhouette of the sniper. Even in the growing darkness surrounding them, she recognized the shadow. The figure took off a baseball cap and waved it before her at the edge of the rooftop. The woman's auburn hair swirled in the breeze, covering her sharp blue eyes.

Susan Metcalf.

CHAPTER TWENTY

"This isn't going to end well for you, Hendricks. You know that, right?" The question came with a spray of blood. Ben's tongue was slick with the thick liquid. Hendricks pawed at the red glommed to his skin.

Ben's question served a second, unseen purpose. Behind his back, Ben's thumb popped from its socket. He choked back the pain it sent through his hand, which in fact was trivial compared to the rest of his wounds. The pain wasn't the issue, though. He needed more time to clear his clouded vision. The trigger-happy fiend responsible for four deaths in the span of ten seconds was not likely to provide it.

Air left him. Another kick landed hard against his sore ribs. Hendricks grinned. "Didn't your mother ever teach you to shut your mouth?"

Ben coughed. More blood dripped from his lips. He struggled to get back on his knees. "She was too busy teaching me right from wrong. You must have skipped that lesson."

"Cute," Hendricks said. His fist shot out, but he paused the strike when Ben attempted to dodge the blow. Satisfied at the fear dominating the wounded agent's lone open eye, Hendricks laughed. "Not for much longer though."

Ben arched his back, fighting for breath. His chest swelled defiantly at the murderer. "You don't have an answer, do you? Sullivan will kill you for this. He's not one to let loose ends slip back into the night."

"He'll make an exception," Hendricks said with a shrug. His interest was fading fast. "I know who he's betraying with this little coup. The Trust aren't the forgiving sort."

The Trust. The name of Sullivan's group. Who else was involved? How far-reaching did this extend? And what came next?

"Besides," Hendricks continued, "he's too busy with his pet project to care."

"The Wellspring," Ben exclaimed. "I know —"

A punch sent Ben reeling, but he refused to fall. He hadn't seen the punch at all. The left side was completely blacked out from the punishment. Hendricks cracked his knuckles with satisfaction.

"You know nothing, Riley. So knock it off with the story. How you learned the damn name is astonishing, but we both know the truth." Hendricks leaned closer, his wide left eye filling Ben's vision. "You'll never understand what the Wellspring represents, or the true threat coming. Not even Sullivan understands that much."

"Feel like sharing?"

"I have been, Riley." Hendricks delivered another punch across Ben's cheek. "Want more?"

Ben's eyes thinned. "Bring it, you sadistic monster."

"Gladly."

The fist flew toward Ben's left side just as he knew it would. He turned to face the imminent blow. Ben snatched Hendricks' arm at the elbow. Using the mercenary's momentum, Ben pivoted and flipped Hendricks into the concrete wall of the Edgemont.

Hendricks' body fell soundly to the floor of the alley. Ben refused to glance back. He searched through the debris of human life for something he could use. Grabbing at a dead man's lost pistol, Ben fled for the front of the building and his freedom.

"Dammit," Hendricks cursed. "Riley!"

The sound of two shots rang through the wind tunnel of the alley. Ben reached the corner just as the first shot missed him by less than an inch to his left. The second connected with the building. Shattered brick sprayed over his face. He tumbled forward, blinded by the brick. He swatted the flakes of debris out of his only good eye, while maintaining a precarious pace.

Once on the street he broke into a full run. He fought through the pain coursing throughout his beaten and bloodied body. At the end of the block he turned north. Heavy footfalls echoed in the air, each one closer than the last. Ben knew Hendricks would never stop chasing after him, never slow in his dogged pursuit until he found his revenge. Ben wanted to catch his breath, but held no guarantee his body would have the strength to start again. He needed to hold on a little longer, push a little harder to make it.

Three blocks east stood an abandoned school; it had been of-fered by Metcalf as a resupply and safehouse if everything went south. The school had closed for budgetary reasons, and the place had been fenced off from the public and utilized by the covert agency as an off-the-books resource.

It had been meant to serve as a refuge. Hendricks, however, had made that impossible. Ben slipped through a small tear along the chain link fence. The broken latch on the side door gave him instant access to the building. He took the stairs two at a time. His legs screamed with each pump as he put as much distance as possible from his pursuer.

His chest heaved. Under the swelling of his cheek he felt sweat pouring down. At the fourth floor of the school, Ben start-ed down the long hallway. From below, the side doors slammed shut once more.

"RILEY!" Hendricks bellowed. More bestial than man, the mercenary was clearly fed up with the chase. Now it was time for the kill.

Dammit.

Ben held tight to the pistol and shuffled to the end of the cor-ridor. The last door on the left opened and he rushed inside. He closed it slowly, the creaking lingering longer instead of lessen-ing. Ben moved for the cubby closet in the corner of the room. He slid it open and a go-bag rested within. Quickly, Ben pulled loose the spare pistol, a Glock 42, and tucked it into his waist-band at the small of his back.

This was meant to be a place to heal, to hide until it was safe to journey out into the world. If anything, it was meant to bring them back together. Morgan and Metcalf. Zac. Hell, even Lincoln if he ever returned to the fold. Ben had served as bait for Sulli-van with the hope of saving them all.

Morgan. The thought of her name caused him to stumble back on his legs. If Metcalf was gone, if she had been unable to fulfill her promise to get everyone else to safety, then what had hap-pened to Morgan? He had pledged to be there for her, to be her partner. After everything he had put her through recently he needed to make good on that promise.

He had to stop Hendricks. No matter the cost.

Footsteps approached rapidly. The mercenary was coming. Without hesitation. Without fear at what might await him. Ben closed the cubby. Steadying himself, he raised his gun to the door of the classroom.

He was trapped and alone. Whenever he had pictured his final moments, it had never been like this. *How did I think this was going to end?*

The door kicked open. Ben fired into the dark, his scream louder than the bullets raging from the barrel of his gun. He emptied the clip in seconds. When his eye readjusted to the room he found nothing in the doorway.

Is he...?

Out of the shadows Hendricks' laughter, proud and dominant, thundered through the room before he stepped inside. His sidearm gleamed in the dim moonlight that peeked through dust-filled windows.

"End of the line."

CHAPTER TWENTY-ONE

Part of her hesitated. As the snow continued to fall lightly on the field, Morgan remained near Grissom's cooling corpse. He had once offered her a second chance. He had pulled her out of the gutter—working in a dank and decrepit nowhere bar. At the time she had had no mission. No purpose. No loved ones. There was little to look forward to in her life. Grissom had saved her. He had changed her world.

She'd repaid him by ending his life a second time.

Slowly, she inched closer until she was right beside him. She crouched down and pulled at Grissom's bulky frame, shifting him until he lay on his back in the field. His eyes no longer glowed their deep blue, natural or otherwise. They were expressionless just like his face.

"God," Morgan muttered. Why couldn't the memory remain? Why couldn't her heroic image of him stay locked in her mind forever, never fading and never forgotten. The truth, however, was that Grissom was a traitor who had been working with another group to subvert the DSA's mission—working against Metcalf for years without her knowing.

Morgan had trusted him.

And he had betrayed that trust with every word spoken, with every operation completed.

Damn you, Jake. She closed his eyes and ran her hand along his cheek and down to his chest. Small bumps of circuitry ran under his skin. His enhancements had created the perfect killing machine. In the center of his chest was a small box, inserted into him like a thumb drive. It appeared to feed into a dozen other channels running throughout his body. A central processing unit.

"What did the Trust do to you?" she whispered. "How could you let this happen? The DSA was your home, your family, and you—"

The DSA isn't what it seems.

How many more times would she have to be reminded before she understood? From how many trusted souls did she have to hear the warning? Ben and Lincoln had both claimed such doubts, yet she'd continued to delude herself; she had believed completely in the work.

Morgan moved to grab the thin unit. Her hands braced against Grissom's cold skin. Her nails dug into flesh that felt like plastic. The thin box pried loose and she held it on her palm like a prize trophy.

She peered into the chasm left in the man's chest in an attempt to probe him for further study, when the sound of screeching tires echoed from the far side of the field. Two police cruisers came to a halt at the edge of the park. The officers vacated their vehicles in a hurry.

It was time to leave.

"Damn." She hesitated a moment longer, hand tight to the small processing unit. A soft-spoken goodbye for her friend escaped into the frigid air. Then she bolted in the opposite direction, rushing for the waiting street to slip into the shadows.

Her feet ached and felt frozen from exposure, but she made it back to the pick-up truck. That was when Morgan found her—down the street more than a hundred yards, crumpled against a building.

Stephanie Atwater. One arm was over her head, and another was bent awkwardly against her back. She wasn't alone. A lean figure wearing a ball cap crouched at her side.

"Metcalf?" Morgan asked. She passed a green compact car parked on the curb with the engine still running.

Metcalf stroked the scraped cheek of the young woman. "She was a good friend."

"She saved my life."

Metcalf smiled, tears clinging to her cheeks. "Mine too. Too often." She took a sharp breath, then faced the woman in the workout clothes. "Grissom?"

"You knew it was him?"

More tears escaped and ran down the length of her cheeks. "Did he say anything to you? Did he—?"

Morgan nodded. "Metcalf, he…"

"It's okay," Metcalf interrupted. "It's okay. We can talk about it later. We should probably…"

"Right."

Metcalf cradled Stephanie close. She tucked her arms under the dead woman to get a good grip as she lifted. "Grab the door for me."

"What are you doing?"

Metcalf's glare slammed into her like a punch. "I'm not leaving her. Not like this."

"Police are inbound," Morgan said, pointing down the block. It would take less than three minutes for the two cruisers to make it to their position from the opposite side of the field. "Metcalf—"

"Help me, Morgan," Metcalf said, eyes pleading for the argument to end. "She deserves better. She deserved *much* better."

Through the tears and the sentimentality, the sense of loss accompanied every word. Metcalf had never connected with her agents, her analysts, or anyone really. Never. She was an objective observer who made the call no one else would. Her cold rationality had constantly made the most difficult decisions.

Now she struggled. Not just in the physical moving of their fallen colleague, but in everything. Stephanie was important to Metcalf—more important than anything Morgan had observed during their time together.

"I've got her," Morgan said. She took the weight from Metcalf. Straining from the day's events, Morgan lifted the young woman's body over her shoulder and shuffled quickly down the sidewalk.

"The car is—"

"I know," Morgan replied. She waited for Metcalf to open the back door before gently laying the deceased in the vehicle. Both took a moment to look at her cradled body in the back seat of the compact car. A prayer slipped from Morgan's lips.

Metcalf moved for the driver's side. The sorrow faded for a moment and her gruff exterior returned. "How many?"

"At least four," Morgan said, slipping into the passenger seat. The sooner they were on the road, the sooner they would be out of the spotlight. No one would notice another car on the street. Not at this hour.

"We need to move, then," Metcalf said. She took a long look through the rearview mirror, checking the street but also hovering over the precious cargo silent in the back. Metcalf shifted the car to drive, then merged with traffic. Morgan slouched along her seat. Metcalf straightened the hat to cover her auburn locks just as the two cruisers sped by them. Neither took a breath for over a minute. Not until the flashing lights faded and the darkness of the countryside became their only company.

"Where?" Morgan asked, staring out into the growing shadows. "Where can we possibly go now?"

Metcalf kept her eyes on the winding path ahead as she pressed harder on the accelerator. "The only place left to us."

CHAPTER TWENTY-TWO

Metcalf remained silent for the drive north of the city. For more than an hour images of the woman in the backseat plagued her thoughts. She wondered what Stephanie had been thinking about in her last moments. Did she blame Metcalf? Did she blame herself? Every thought forced her hands to tighten on the wheel of the car. Her foot braced against the accelerator, pushing the four-cylinder faster down the dark stretch of highway.

There was no one else to blame for what happened—no one else to look to for comfort. It fell on her. It had been her call to send Stephanie into the field to retrieve Morgan. It was a simple-enough request immediately compromised by Sullivan's forces. When the plan had fallen apart, when the call came from Stephanie for assistance, she had taken her position on the roof. She had hidden in the shadows while others took the risk and waited for her shot, only to find Grissom at the end of her scope.

She had ended his life for a second time; it was another judgment call made without hesitation. She prided herself on being a leader and on having foresight. She had never seen him coming. She had never realized the extent to which she might fall, thanks to Sullivan's machinations. She had been branded a traitor side-by-side with her field team. Nothing could have prepared her for the events of the day. Now it was too late, and she had pulled the trigger on the man who had stood at her side from the beginning.

Even having rescued Morgan there was no sense of success in her eyes. Her failure to anticipate Sullivan's plans overshadowed their survival. It was a failure that would never fade from her memory, no matter how many times she tucked it within her lockbox and closed the lid.

Unfortunately, she had to put all distractions away for the time being. She forced herself to close off all emotion; she had to swallow all thoughts other than the mission. Sullivan had made his move. The time had come to regroup and recover.

The snow steadily pounded against the windshield. They turned left at Odenton and made for the Pennsylvania border near the edge of West Virginia. Farm country took over the scenery.

The compact car shifted from the main road, making for the large country home on the left. The property ran across several acres of land. Behind the home there was an apple orchard. The place had not been kept up for some time by the looks of it. The home carried shattered windows along the front edifice. Loosely hung shutters slammed against the bubbled siding. The car passed along the dirt road that served as the driveway for the property.

"What is this place?" Morgan asked.

"My retirement home," Metcalf whispered, waiting for the eventual follow-up question. None came and the silence gave her time to collect her thoughts. The car coasted through the drifts of snow toward a small hillside behind the orchard and tucked out of sight. The back half bled into a frozen pond at the end of the property line, but the front interested Metcalf more. The entire face was carved out with a large metal door positioned within the opening.

This was her safe place; it was one she had imagined would carry her to old age—sitting on the porch and watching the sunset, as if dreams such as those were ever truly achieved. Over time the notion had faded. Her tenure at the DSA always demanded more and more time to ever consider retirement. Her absence from the home had offered her the chance to turn the property into something else.

The car slowed to a halt. Metcalf and Morgan exited the vehicle, both taking a moment to pause at the back seat. Without a word, they started for the metal door. Metcalf took the lead. Morgan trailed her closely.

"The Bunker," Metcalf announced. She opened a small metal box beside the embedded door. After she inputted a ten-digit code the door groaned to life, and it shuffled the snow out of its path as it opened. "The name of this place is the Bunker."

"Got a story to go with that name?" Morgan asked as she limped into the cavernous entryway.

Metcalf followed behind, moving to the right of the inner chamber. The inside looked like a metal cylinder complete with a lustrous floor beneath them. Small lights embedded along the sides of the hill illuminated the solitary room. The only other fixture in the structure was a small panel in the wall next to the door. It contained another keypad, similar to the one outside, as well as a hand scanner. Metcalf placed her right hand on the surface and punched in a secondary trigger code. She stepped back as her identity was confirmed across the readout in bold letters.

"A last resort."

The floor shook and Morgan struggled to steady herself. The lights on the side of the wall slowly shifted higher as the floor descended deeper into the earth. Lighting ran along the walls. The elevator picked up speed. Morgan closed her eyes until at last the ride came to an end.

A new set of doors opened behind them, LED's flickering to life overhead in a straight line. The corridor held many of the same properties as the DSA warehouse. Concrete walls and floors. Support beams to keep the hill above them from collapsing. No decoration, no pomp, just functionality for the task ahead. A single door rested at the end of the hall.

Morgan hesitated when Metcalf ushered her on. "It was designed as a failsafe in case everything fell apart."

Scanners clicked upon her approach. The readout ran beside the lone door at the end of the corridor. Security systems maintained the secrecy even within the structure.

"Being labeled a traitor by your own agency seems to qualify."

Metcalf nodded. "I kept the place off the books. It was mine, but DSA resources made it more."

Morgan huffed. "Secrets within secrets."

"That is how the game is played," Metcalf responded. Her answer had been far too casual given their day. She regretted her choice of words instantly, but kept her eyes on the keypad next to the last entry point. Morgan made her disdain self-evident with each breath.

"How's that working out for you?" Morgan snapped, unable

to let the comment slide. "You should have told me. I believed in you. I believed in what we were doing at the DSA. How could you let us be manipulated by the Trust?"

"Where… Where did you hear that name?"

"It was…" Morgan's gaze fell. "It doesn't matter. I should have known this crap with Sullivan was happening."

If Metcalf had brought her people in sooner, if she had found some way to reach out to them and to trust them, would things have changed? Would Stephanie still be alive? Would the DSA still be under threat and out of reach from her if she had acted instead of waiting for Sullivan? She didn't know, and the thought destroyed her inside.

"You're right," she said. Her head fell to her chest and she quietly entered the command code on the pad.

"Damn right I am," Morgan pressed. A hand snatched Metcalf's shoulder and twisted her away from the panel. Morgan held six inches over the director, forcing Metcalf to look up into her brown eyes. "Admitting it just makes the whole damn thing worse."

Metcalf's eyes thinned. "I said you were right. Don't push it."

"Open the door, Metcalf."

The barrier unlocked with a loud hiss. Metcalf stepped aside to make room for her company. "Make yourself at home," Metcalf said. "We could be here a while."

Morgan stopped at the entrance and took in the space. Slight awe followed the tall woman's gaze. Before them was a briefing area, including a conference table and computer terminals. A series of monitors to keep track of events hung above the work stations. Currently on the main board in the middle of the area was a task bar working its way to completion.

To the left of the entrance, the kitchen area extended thirty feet deep and twelve feet wide with tables positioned along the wall opposite the counter space. Freezer units were positioned in the back beside a pantry stocked for at least three nuclear winters if need be. Weapons closets and supplies occupied a series of storage compartments to the right.

Twin corridors branched from the sides of the common area. These led to dormitory units. There was space for fifty souls in the bunker, though Metcalf couldn't imagine the number of residents would ever reach anywhere near that level. Branches ran from the living quarters, including training facilities, laundry machines, and the mainframes for the extensive computer network contained beneath the hillside.

The exhausted woman leaned on the counter that stretched into the kitchen; she felt relief fill her when the door to the bunker closed completely. Guilt kept the calm from penetrating too deep. The price had been too great. Her friend had deserved better.

Morgan made it halfway through the room before her arms spread in exclamation. "You hid this from everyone? How?"

"I'm very good at my job. Or I was," Metcalf said. "Dorms are to the back. Kitchen and pantry right here, of course." Metcalf pointed to the screen to the back of the bunker. "The Archive should be fully integrated soon."

"Metcalf—"

The former director stared at the crawling status bar. Her sullen gaze searched the entire area, taking in her surroundings: the setup of foodstuffs, the full cabinetry with utensils, and the tools and supplies littering the compartments to the right.

Her head fell to her chest, a hand over her brow. "Stephanie was able… She took care of it all for us. For me."

"Listen…"

Metcalf waved her off. "I knew Sullivan was coming for me, Morgan. *Me.* Stephanie helped fake my death and take me off the board, so that you would be safe from him. I didn't think things would get this bad."

"What is he after?"

"Something I've been looking into for years," Metcalf said. She slipped the rifle from her shoulder and set it in the corner of the room. A series of duffel bags were tucked by the railing that cut the entryway from the briefing area. "I kept the files secured, locked away from him, but it's only a matter of time."

"I know who could help with that," Morgan said, pointing at the computer equipment stacked throughout. She moved for the dormitories.

"Morgan—"

"I'll get Zac and we'll…" Morgan trailed off as Metcalf's gaze lowered to the floor. "You grabbed Zac, didn't you? He's here, right?"

"Morgan." Metcalf took a deep breath. The former director of the DSA removed her ball cap and straightened her hair, fighting for the right words. "I know about you two. You need to understand. I don't mean for this to sound—"

Morgan rushed toward her, frustration mounting. "Where is he?"

Metcalf raised her hands in defense, then let them fall. Morgan grabbed Susan's coat and pulled her close. Their eyes locked. "With Sullivan."

"No." Morgan shook her head. She stepped back, hands still balled in fists. "No way. He wouldn't—"

"He's been working with Sullivan for weeks," Metcalf continued. "Planting bugs in my office. He hacked my emails and removed priority updates from my system. They even monitored your apartment."

Morgan's eyes widened. "He wouldn't... We—"

"Morgan, please." Metcalf started down the metal stairs to the operations area. She queued up a small terminal along the conference table. "We were able to loop into the feed from the warehouse. It's time delayed to keep suspicion to a minimum. I caught this from my mobile earlier."

The feed came up and displayed Sullivan's hand clasped tight to Zac's shoulder. The image was enough to drive Metcalf's point home with the confused and overwhelmed agent. Her knuckles blanched from her grip on the railing above.

"Treason?" Zac's question echoed through the speakers.

"They've been working against the agency," Sullivan said. *"Working to subvert our attempts to learn more about the Bellbrook incident, about the men responsible for the Promethean project you uncovered in Chicago and more. Lincoln's actions alone warrant investigation into their practices."*

"Sir?"

"I know how this sounds, Zac. I need to know if you're still with me."

His hesitation lasted only a moment. "I'm with you, sir. I'll do whatever it takes."

Metcalf killed the monitor and ended the captured conversation. Morgan's head fell to her chest.

"It can't be," Morgan muttered. "Zac would never betray us."

"He did," Metcalf said, the words sharp. She needed Morgan back with her. She had to know if Morgan's loyalty had wavered. Her reaction to the recording confirmed it for Metcalf, even though the choice pained her. "Come on, Morgan. What else could he do?"

"He could have come here!" Morgan yelled. "To your damn bunker."

"To be labeled as a traitor like us? He has a family."

Morgan's jaw clenched. She screamed, throwing her hands from the railing. They slammed along her thighs repeatedly until her head bowed in surrender. "I know."

Morgan rubbed at her eyes. Metcalf moved to her, then stopped. "I'm sorry."

"I doubt it."

"I deserve that," Metcalf said with a slight nod. "Like I said, get comfortable. There are clothes for you down the hall to the right. Then we can start figuring this out."

She didn't bother to wait for the argument to continue. Instead, Metcalf entered the supply closet. She pulled loose a shovel hanging beside the door and clutched tight to the handle. Part of her had hoped to put it off, to let the task slip into the background, to take the work head on and get lost in it. Stephanie came first. That was how it always should have been. Stephanie had earned that much, albeit far too late to appreciate the gesture.

Morgan blocked the door when she returned.

"What?"

"Don't make me ask." Morgan crossed her arms, refusing to budge. "You've avoided talking about him this whole time. He's obviously part of this crap you've pulled me into, so where is he? Where is Riley?"

Metcalf attempted to push through, keeping her head low. "He's not coming."

"The keys," Morgan said. She continued to stonewall Metcalf. "Now."

Metcalf didn't flinch. "No."

"That wasn't a request."

Metcalf squeezed the handle of the shovel. "Doesn't change the answer."

"Riley's alone out there," Morgan snapped. "No phone. No gun. Out there, because of your power struggle with Sullivan. I won't leave him behind."

"I did what I could for him," Metcalf replied. "It was his choice, Morgan."

"What? What do you mean?" Metcalf didn't want the fight. Neither of them needed another argument, especially after their day. Metcalf waited, holding back until the anger faded from the face of the woman begging for a fight. Realization crept in, and Morgan's muscles slackened. "He knew."

"In Buffalo. I told him what I could."

Morgan held the wall, struggling to stay upright. "And he chose what? To play the sacrificial lamb? He wanted to be bait for Sullivan? What?"

"Yes," Metcalf answered. She moved close to Morgan, giving the confused agent a half smile. "He made a request. If it came down to it, if there was only one that could be saved…"

"He wanted it to be me." Morgan punched the wall. "That idiot. That—"

"I did what I could for him," Metcalf said. "But it was his choice."

"It was a mistake."

Metcalf gripped the shovel tighter. They all had plenty of mistakes on the tally for the day. "It was still his to make." Her hand fell on Morgan's. "Ben is on his own."

CHAPTER TWENTY-THREE

Ben threw the empty pistol at Hendricks, forcing the scarred mercenary to duck to avoid the projectile aimed at his head. Hendricks stared in disbelief. He watched the weapon as it clattered across the hall before skittering out of sight. When he returned his focus to the room he was more surprised at what followed up the pistol.

Ben himself.

With only a second to react, Hendricks took a single shot. His gun was off target thanks to his position in the doorway. His eyes had not fully adjusted to the darkness of the abandoned school, which was what Ben was counting on when he blitzed toward the man.

The shot hit the charging man's right bicep, causing a wave of pain to ripple through his wounded and broken body. Still he pressed forward, pushing his legs harder, forcing them to move faster before Hendricks could take another shot. Ben screamed, and the sound bounced through the connecting hallways. With every ounce of strength left in him, Ben threw his body at the mercenary. Both slammed into the ground hard. Ben refused to let his wounded arm slow him down, even with the fresh stream of blood running off his elbow and onto the floor below.

"That's right, Riley," Hendricks sneered in a half smile, his left side refusing to cooperate. He kneed Ben's torso hard, then tossed him to the side. "Show me who you really are."

Ben struggled to get back up from the tile floor. The blow had done more damage than he was willing to admit. He needed to stand. He needed to move. Focusing on everything other than the pain, Ben lunged back at Hendricks. The two collided, sending them back into the open classroom at the end of the fourth floor. They kicked and clawed at each other as they rolled along the dust-littered tile.

"You sure know how to show a guy a good time, Riley," Hendricks said with a laugh. He dodged Ben's sloppy blows before delivering a chop to the back of his neck. Hendricks circled his bloodied prey. He exuded confidence and strength. Ben, though, fought a losing battle on two fronts: one internally and the one in front of him. "You know, I got a look at the real you in Buffalo. Felt great letting all that anger out, didn't it?"

"You were there?" Ben asked, wondering what could have connected Hendricks with that case. Then he recalled what else had happened during his stay. "No."

"Yeah," Hendricks muttered with a shrug.

"Horace Waters." The man who had ruined Ben's career in Buffalo—who had taken his entire life away in a single day. The man who had died from an apparent suicide the same day Ben returned to the city. Sullivan was behind the act, though Ben had never thought for a second that the old man hired the job out to someone else. Ben should have known better.

"He was not your biggest fan." Hendricks licked his lips. His fists tightened, ready for the next blow. "I actually kinda liked him. Oh well."

"Dammit, Hendricks!" Ben screamed, the anger and the humiliation of it all boiling over in him. "Damn you!"

Ben leapt at the man. Hendricks sidestepped the assault. He drove his fists down hard on Ben's back, sending the beaten agent of the DSA to the ground. Hendricks goaded him with each false start, but Ben refused to quit. He clawed and scratched his way to his knees before pulling up his tired body with the help of a nearby desk.

Hendricks pulled his gun up from the floor, then leveled it on the bleeding agent. A single shot thundered in Ben's ear. The blast stung in his gut. A small puncture wound stained his shirt. He choked on words of defiance, a last joke to share with the triumphant murderer.

The mercenary wasn't finished with him, however. Hendricks grabbed Ben's throat and lifted him from the floor. Pulling Ben close, he whispered in his ear, "Guess you never had what it takes after all, Riley. Maybe next time around."

Without thought, without effort, Hendricks threw the weightless victim at the filth-laden row of windows lining the classroom. Ben felt lighter than air as his body soared into the glass and shattered the thin pane. The night wind rushed around him, cool and refreshing.

Then the fall truly began.

CHAPTER TWENTY-FOUR

Things had changed. One month had slipped by since Lincoln's last day at the DSA warehouse. It was the day he had received his final assignment, an assignment he had failed to complete. When he'd last spoken with the young Head of Operational Support and Research, Lincoln had berated him. Zac was eight years his junior, yet acted as if he owned the place. It wasn't the arrogance Lincoln minded, it was the fact that the arrogance was a poorly veiled attempt to hide his fear.

Now, no fear sat in the young man's eyes. Upon recognizing Lincoln's arrival and noticing the weapon pointed at him, there was only one emotion on display. Pity. Not concern for his safety or those around him, nor terror at the threat in their midst. Only sadness for the man holding the gun.

Lincoln preferred fear; he preferred anything but what stood before him.

"I'll listen better without the gun," Zac said, hands raised and open in defense. "Promise."

Lincoln remembered the stutter in his speech from their last briefing together. That had been before Bellbrook. Every time Zac had caught Lincoln playing with a bullet from his service weapon, his lips had frozen. That fear, however instinctive, had apparently departed during their time apart.

"Wish I could, kid," Lincoln said. A single duffel bag was strapped tight to his back. He left the other tucked behind the toilet and closed the stall door. "Where's Sullivan?"

"Lincoln, this doesn't have to—"

The gun settled along Zac's sweating brow. Lincoln's shadow swallowed him whole. "I'm not here to hurt you, Modine. Take me to Sullivan and I'm gone. Simple."

"Our definitions of simple must differ," Zac muttered. He glanced at the door. Hope rested in Zac's wayward gaze. Lincoln knew if Zac cried out there was a chance members of the research team might hear him. Lincoln didn't give him the chance. He spun Zac around and prodded him forward for the waiting hall. "Lincoln, listen—"

"Not interested."

"He's branded you a traitor. You, the field team… and Metcalf."

"Not my concern."

"You already know?"

Lincoln pulled the door open and shoved Zac into the corridor. "Guy I'm working with stays pretty well-informed."

"The Witness? Lincoln, you can't possibly trust—"

"Don't," Lincoln growled. He didn't need the lecture, but what interested him more was the concern in Zac's voice. Even with a gun pointed at him, Zac played the protector—the worried friend.

"All right, all right." Zac held up his hands. The hall remained empty, but Lincoln continued to edge him closer to the janitor's closet around the corner and out of sight. The kid hesitated.

Lincoln jammed the gun into Zac's back. "I don't have time for games, Modine. Where the hell is he?"

"Seriously, Lincoln, this isn't—"

Lincoln yanked Zac's arm down then twisted it high against his back until he cried out from the strain. "Where?"

"All right," the kid whispered through gritted teeth. Tears of pain joined the sweat on his cheeks. Lincoln relaxed his grip slightly and stepped away. His eyes softened. Zac rubbed his arm. "The Archive, Lincoln. He's in the Archive."

Lincoln nodded. Reaching for the right wall adjacent to the dead-end closet, Lincoln pushed against a small panel at the base of the wall. The wall receded and a hidden door opened. Inside was a single ladder heading both up and down through the structure. Zac stared blankly, searching the area.

"So that's how Adler did it."

"Who?"

"Doesn't matter."

"That's right," Lincoln said. The gun returned to his captive's back. "Now lead the way."

"Great." Zac's head slumped. He grabbed the closest rung and started down to the lower level of the warehouse.

It took a while for them to reach the sub-basement. Zac maintained a snail's pace, careful with each rung descending deeper into the structure. Lincoln's sidearm tracked him the entire way, ready for the slightest move by the kid. He couldn't take any chances.

"Zac, listen… I'm not…" Lincoln hesitated when they arrived at the lowest level of the warehouse. He stood before the wall of remembrance for those fallen. His eyes fell on Ruth Heller's plaque. "I haven't lost sight of anything, Modine. I haven't forgotten why I'm doing this."

Zac stopped, following his eyes to the plaques on the wall. "Are you trying to convince me or yourself? Or her? Either way, the strong-arm tactics aren't helping your argument."

Lincoln nodded, ushering Zac forward. The gun proved to be sufficient motivation for the tech. "This Wellspring thing is dangerous. Sullivan doesn't get that. He's manipulating the DSA and twisting everything we've ever done, all for his own ends. Even you, Zac. You have to see that. *He's* the traitor here."

"Simple as that?" Zac asked in disbelief. Stopping in front of the Archive door, he turned to face the man. "Lincoln, listen —"

"No." Lincoln shook his head.

"Yeah. That's what I thought," Zac huffed. He stared at Lincoln as a stranger would; they were no longer colleagues, no longer fighting the same fight for the same goal. "Want me to open the door?"

Next to the door was an electronic keypad. Unique access codes were given out to each and every member of the team with clearance for the room. The same code was used at their terminals for electronic access, which allowed the system to recognize who was viewing what and when.

Zac moved for the keypad. Lincoln stopped him, fingers digging into the kid's arm. "Your code. Got it?"

"I figured," Zac replied. He left the keypad exposed so Lincoln could witness his entry. A series of six numbers was entered slowly. The door clicked open from the frame. Lincoln used the gun to prod Zac into the room before following a step behind.

There were staging tables front and center as they entered. Beyond them, rows of filing cabinets led into the darkness. The room was empty of personnel. No one sifted through documents. There wasn't a single analyst or tech present. And definitely no Sullivan.

"Where the hell is he?" Lincoln snapped.

Zac held out his hands, backing away until he hit one of the tables. "Lincoln—"

"I'm not playing around, Modine!" Lincoln yelled, both hands clamped tight to his gun. "Bring me Sullivan now."

"So you can kill him? Just like you did with those guys in Des Moines? Is that what you are now? A hired gun?"

"I am trying to save us. All of us."

"Are you really?" The tech stepped deeper into the room. Lincoln trailed his movements. "Come on, Lincoln. Talk to me. Drop the gun and—"

His hands were at Zac's collar before his next breath. He charged for the wall, slamming the overweight analyst against a closed filing cabinet. "Last time. Don't make me do this."

"No, Agent MacKenzie," a voice called from the open door. Both turned for the entry point and the shadow of Greg Sullivan. His hands were clasped behind his back. "You will not be doing anything except what Zac has asked. Put the gun down."

"Director," Zac called. "I tried to—"

"The door," Lincoln interrupted. He let go of Zac and raised the pistol at the man he had been sent to kill. "That code you entered. It was some kind of signal?"

Zac nodded. "I was hoping to talk to you, hoping you would hear me and see that what you're doing goes against everything you believe in. You aren't some mindless killer. That isn't you, Lincoln."

Lincoln's eyes thinned. All it would take was a single shot right between the eyes and it would be over. Mission accomplished. Another man would be dead by his hand. Then what? There would always be another mission, another death for the sake of the future—the unseen and glorious world to come.

"This isn't about me, Zac," he said, hesitant against the trigger. His words ricocheted in the emptiness of the space. They echoed between his ears as he made his decision. His finger left the trigger entirely. "It can't be about me. This is about Sullivan and what he intends to do next."

"Indeed it is," Sullivan said. He raised his right hand and the weapon in its grasp.

"Wait, this doesn't have to —"

Two shots cut through Zac's words. The researcher's bright eyes widened in terror. Heat rose from Lincoln's chest and his back.

"Lincoln?" Zac reached out to catch the falling agent. Lincoln's gun dropped to the ground with a clatter. His hands rushed to his chest and the growing stain slipping through the vest. Air left his lungs as his body joined his weapon on the floor.

"Lincoln!" Zac cried. Blood trickled beneath Lincoln and pooled atop from the gaping wounds through his Kevlar vest.

"Zac..."

"I'm sorry. I didn't..."

Lincoln nodded. "You were right, Zac. I... couldn't do it. Not again."

"You have to believe me, Lincoln," Zac pleaded. "I had no choice."

"Don't explain yourself, Zac," Sullivan declared, stepping deeper into the room.

The small pistol in his hand reflected the light overhead. A FN Five-seven — Lincoln couldn't help but take note of the weapon, even with the pain coursing through him. It used armor-piercing rounds that had cut through his body armor like it was made of paper. *Damn Belgians.* Lincoln fought for breath as shadows fell over him.

Greg Sullivan smiled. "Agent MacKenzie knew *exactly* how this was going to end."

CHAPTER TWENTY-FIVE

He had made this happen. When Zac had punched in the panic code, a single digit off from his own, he had brought this fate down on the man he had never once considered a friend. The non-stop badgering and berating given by Lincoln had made it clear where their relationship lay in his mind. To Zac, though, there was never a question. They served the same purpose, worked toward the same goal. He had never imagined it would end like this—that he would be the cause of so much pain.

Yet that was exactly what had happened. Zac's good intentions, his dedication to Sullivan's team, had made this possible: two bullets and a slow death for Lincoln MacKenzie.

"I detest these things," Sullivan said, displaying the weapon. "But it pays to be prepared, doesn't it? Something with enough firepower for those pesky vests you tend to wear."

"You're one to talk about vests," Lincoln muttered, followed by a string of thick coughs. Zac bent closer, his hands firmly on the two spouting wounds along Lincoln's chest. His actions made no difference; no amount of pressure would have any effect at this point.

"Enough chit chat, then, I take it?" Sullivan asked. He pulled a chair over and sat in front of the pair, his sidearm dangling casually at his side. "Very well. You're going to tell me everything you know about the man you call the Witness. You are going to tell me who he is, as well as his current location. Then you are going to share his plans for the Wellspring and this facility. You will do this now, and you will live. That is my promise to you, Agent MacKenzie."

"Like hell," Lincoln laughed. More blood spilled from his lips and dribbled down his chin. His eyes never strayed from the director. His bloodshot orbs never blinked, never showed the fear behind them.

Sullivan smirked. "You have no conception of the resources at my disposal. A doctor is no stretch."

Lincoln fought to sit upright, then steadied his head to spit in Sullivan's direction. "Pass."

"Lincoln," Zac whispered. He caught Sullivan's glare out of his periphery. The bleeding was increasing. Lincoln's dark skin paled under the Archive room lights. Lincoln held out his hand, took Zac's, and squeezed.

"Leave, Modine," Lincoln said, the words exasperated. "You don't want to be here for this."

Zac shook his head. "Director, please. You stopped him. That's enough."

"Hardly. Remember, Zac, you helped make this possible."

He didn't need the reminder. He had used his alert code to betray Lincoln. He had been trying to save Sullivan, but it all added up to the same in the end. Lincoln dragged Zac close.

"It's all right, kid."

"I didn't know," Zac replied.

"We never do."

"Answer him. Save your life, Lincoln. Please."

"Listen to him, Lincoln," Sullivan said disdainfully. He sat back in his chair, clearly disinterested in their conversation. He had already asked his questions, it seemed. If they were answered it was to his benefit, but if not they wouldn't affect his current course. Zac realized it was a win for Sullivan and the DSA no matter what. "The Witness is fighting against a rushing tide. He's trying to stop the inevitable. This is our chance to even the odds and strengthen our position. All you have to do is give him up."

Betray him. To Zac it was a simple equation. Life always outweighed death. Maybe it was a lack of inner strength, or conviction, or some other crap spouted by those with the qualities inherent to make the right decision no matter what the circumstances. Zac only knew that when it came down to it, life won out.

Zac leaned close. "He's not worth dying for, Lincoln. You

know that, right?"

Lincoln forced a smile, his breathing rapid and shallow. "Gotta choose a side, kid. It's all about loyalty now."

Sullivan howled with laughter. "When did you learn to tell a joke, Agent MacKenzie?"

Zac pulled away from the bleeding figure on the floor. He stood and staggered deeper into the room. His cheeks were covered in dried tears, though he'd failed to notice them before. His hands were stained with the blood of the man on the ground.

Lincoln's hand moved to his vest and the chest pocket. "I've got your punchline right here, Sullivan."

Sullivan shook his head, tsking loudly. He left the comfort of his chair without concern. Slow, deliberate movements carried him toward Lincoln, whose hand continued to inch to the pocket for his spare weapon. Sullivan observed the desperate act, then he sighed. "Allow me, Lincoln."

Zac watched in horror, yet he said nothing. He did nothing. Sullivan leveled his gun at Lincoln's head. The end came quick without another word from the two men. A single shot and it was over.

The moment would never fade from view, and Zac knew the never-ending nightmare would wait for him every night for as long as he lived. But he would live. For Lincoln MacKenzie, though, it was well and truly over. There would be no more burning questions. No more betrayals of conscience. There would be nothing more for the former agent of the DSA.

His war had finally ended.

CHAPTER TWENTY-SIX

The scalding water soothed her frozen body. Morgan hated the relaxing sensation it caused along her tense muscles and cracked skin. The bath was a luxury, but a necessary one. Hours spent running around Bethesda in little more than a workout bra and sweatpants had left her shivering and in the throes of hypothermia. Adrenaline had most likely saved her life. Her arguments with Metcalf had served their purpose twofold, keeping her focused on something other than the pain running through her toes and allowing her to make her opinion known.

The bath helped her recover that much faster. She waded in the warm liquid and her shivering slowly faded. She was grateful for the reprieve but knew her time was limited. She had to get moving. She only hoped she wasn't too late.

Silence filled the bunker when she removed her tired and aching form from the water. A thick towel covered her hair and she wrapped another around her waist to lock in the heat.

She was grateful to have made it to the bunker. Despite the enmity about Ben's decision, and Zac's betrayal, she finally felt whole again, especially since she had weather-appropriate clothes to wear. The socks alone sent waves of pleasure through her when she slipped on the thickest set found in the dormitory drawer. A heavy black turtleneck, black pants, and leather coat completed the look. Black on top of black—on top of more black—was not her typical style, but the choices that had been procured by Stephanie in preparation for their extended stay at the bunker were limited at best.

All her choices were limited now. Everything had been stripped away and taken from her. She had no way to contact her family without putting them in the line of fire. Her apartment had been set alight, the site of a double homicide no doubt being blamed on her. She had no way to say otherwise without risking a death squad of DSA Security Division agents. Work was a lie and it always had been. She was still struggling to fathom it. Zac stood on the other side of things, the safer side to be sure, but the wrong side. Or so she hoped.

She pulled the strap of a large duffel bag tighter to her shoulder. Morgan left the confines of the washroom and entered the hall, vacating the room that had been designated for her by Metcalf during her impromptu tour. It was quaint. There was a desk, a bed, and little else in the way of amenities other than the dresser filled with clothes.

Passing through the dormitory area, she noticed other rooms stocked to match her own. The same generic styles made it impossible to gauge the personnel in question but it was clear more people were coming. Not that it mattered to the woman decked out in black. She continued through the corridor and then headed for the exit, leaving behind the underground bunker for the cold outside.

The sting of the winter air hit her hard, but she pushed through the stiff wind without complaint. Tucking the jacket close against her skin, Morgan turned from the dirt road and the waiting car to the hillside. A small light glowed beyond the ridge at the rear of the property. The former director busily dug against the frozen ground. Her heaving breaths of exertion in a steady rhythm masked Morgan's approach to the small clearing over the ridge.

Morgan's foot slipped on the piling snow, and she stumbled on a stump jutting out of the earth. When she steadied herself, she glanced back to get a better look at the obstacle. It wasn't a stump, as she'd first assumed.

It was a grave. Morgan stared at the headstone. It was unmarked from what little light the lantern offered. The question of who the grave belonged to begged to be asked, but she held it back. The grave matched the one currently being completed beside it: Stephanie Atwater's final resting place. Morgan gave the sign of the cross, then straightened the marker she had accidentally disturbed, letting the body buried beneath her feet rest with the query at the tip of her tongue.

Metcalf piled the dirt into the hole. She wiped the sweat along her face with each scoop of the shovel. When she realized Morgan had joined her, the woman with the auburn hair jammed the shovel into the ground.

"The Archive is all set," Morgan said. Her eyes stayed fixed on the second grave.

Metcalf did the same. "Good. That's good."

Goodbyes never came easy for Morgan, a fact she discovered when she fought so hard for her brother's life during the war. To see the grave already dug, the body buried without ceremony, saddened her. Tears dotted her vision and she swiped at them. Morgan suddenly realized what her brother went through daily, knowing three men had died so he could live. That had been her decision at the time. This time, however, the choice had been forced upon her. She was going to have to live with it—or try to, anyway.

"She respected you," Morgan said, needing to break the silence. She needed to not think for a moment. Otherwise, both would be lost in grief and memory. "Looked up to you."

"She was a fool, then," Metcalf replied. Her eyes were reflection pools in the darkness. "A great fool."

"She would have made a top-notch field agent. I'm proud to have worked with her."

"Me too," Metcalf said. "Thank—" She stopped at the sight of the bag over Morgan's shoulder. Susan's muscles tensed immediately, and the dirt-covered superior straightened her back. "What is this?"

"You know what this is."

Metcalf ran her gloved hands through her hair. "It isn't safe right now. First we deal with Sullivan, and then we can—"

"*You* can," Morgan interrupted, unwilling to debate. Too much time had passed as it was, and she cursed the heat that still billowed from her chest thanks to her bath. She hadn't heard from Ben in almost twelve hours, not since their arrival at Dulles. He was alone out there. "You and whoever else you've managed to pull into this."

"I—"

"Doesn't matter why you didn't tell me. I hope they can help."

"They will," Metcalf said. "But I need you here, Morgan. I

can't—"

"Don't," Morgan shot back. "Don't put it on me. Not now."

"Morgan. If I could have saved him, I would have."

"He gave you the out and you took it," Morgan said. She understood the ease in Metcalf's decision thanks to Ben. She could even hear him using the words. After Buffalo, Ben had been in a bad place: guilt-ridden over hurting her in his rage, even though it hadn't been his own. Morgan had recognized his pain and brushed it off, refusing to let the incident cloud their budding partnership. She should have kept a closer eye on him. She should have talked him through it—been there for him as he had with her time and time again. "I can't do that. He sure as hell wouldn't do that to me. Even though I deserve it, the way I've pushed him."

"Listen to me, Morgan. Sullivan—"

"Is your mess. And he's not worth the life of one of our own. Self-preservation is one thing, but not at the expense of losing who we are. Who we're supposed to be." They both fell silent. It was about more than just Ben's life. It was the grave before them and every other death marking their past. Stephanie Atwater. Jacob Grissom—the man Metcalf remembered and the idealized version buried in Morgan's memory. So much death surrounded them, all for a brighter tomorrow that seemed to darken with each turn. They had lost so much, not just in the world, but of themselves during their tenure at the DSA. It was time to get something back.

"Even at the risk of losing everything?"

Morgan bent low. She gathered the broken earth and cradled it close. She let the dirt pour from her grasp over her lost colleague. "Turn our backs on what we value, on our friends, and we lose everything. Riley taught me that."

Metcalf knelt on the opposite side of the grave, head bowed in respect. Her hand rested on the ground. With eyes closed she muttered something under her breath. The words were simple enough to read from the sadness in her face.

Goodbye.

"Morgan," Metcalf said as she stood. She moved toward her coat which rested in the snow nearby. When turned back she held the keys to the car. "There's a resupply near his apartment. You might want to start there."

Metcalf tossed the keys into Morgan's waiting hand. They dangled between her fingers. "Thanks."

"Be careful."

Morgan's lip curled. "Like that's even an option in this line of work."

CHAPTER TWENTY-SEVEN

He may as well have pulled the trigger himself. Zac knelt beside Lincoln's body, unable to look at the fallen soldier. The man had asked for loyalty, he had trusted in Zac to make the right choice, and he had died because of that misplaced trust.

Sullivan holstered the pistol, unable to wipe the satisfaction from his face. He paced the room, the sound of static from the walkie talkie at his belt. He moved on from the death at his feet and carried about his day without a thought to what he left behind.

Zac shook his head, anger welling with his unending tears. "It didn't have to be this way."

"I told him that," Sullivan said.

"No." Zac rushed at the man. Sullivan's eyes widened in surprise. His hand reached for his pistol. Zac forced the hand away and slammed it up and against the wall alongside the other. "Don't play it like that. Don't lie to me, sir. I called you. I put him here for you. You could have subdued him."

Sullivan grinned. "What, you thought I would break out my old wrestling moves from high school? Face reality."

Zac squeezed harder. "Your security team—"

"Was occupied," Sullivan said. He paused, waiting for the anger to drain from the young man's face. He demanded his release with a piercing gaze. Zac obliged, then stepped away. He slammed his hands down on the nearest table. The body was still there. Lincoln was still in the room.

It's all about loyalty now.

He had pledged his to Sullivan. He had promised to continue the work to keep his family—no matter their current situation—

safe from harm's way. From a traitor's end. The price for his loyalty was mounting, though, and it threatened to bury him in the cost.

"You may feel guilty," Sullivan said. He rubbed at his wrists as he shuffled for the door. "I do as well, though you might not believe that. It's natural. He was our friend and colleague. Unfortunately, he became a threat. What do you think he would have done to you had I not shown up?"

Zac feared the answer. He had ever since Lincoln arrived. Lincoln had been his colleague, a valued member of the team. But when he surprised Zac in the men's room, when he pointed that gun at him and made his demands, Zac knew the truth. No matter how much he fought against it now that the man was dead. "He… He wouldn't have—"

Sullivan stopped Zac's stammering. "He was a killer, Zac. You know that as well as I."

Lincoln had said as much. He killed two in Des Moines. He had murdered for his country during multiple tours. Metcalf had sent him after the Witness for that very reason. So when it came down to it, why had he hesitated when Sullivan arrived? He had lowered his gun, and he had failed to add another death to the long list waiting him at the pearly gates. Why?

A hand fell on Zac's shoulders. Sullivan pulled him gently toward the door. "Time to go."

"Where?"

"You tell me," Sullivan said. "Have you unlocked the files?"

The pair exited for the hall, but Zac remained in the shadow of the Archive, unable to leave completely. His fights with Metcalf paled compared to this. What was he hoping to gain by arguing with Sullivan? A clearing of his conscience—some way to assuage the guilt over everything? He had made so many mistakes lately.

Was this another one?

"Zac?" Sullivan called. He stood before the plaques of the fallen, though he didn't glance in their direction. Not like Lincoln had when he passed. Sullivan worried too much about the future to give a damn about what came before.

This was where Zac's loyalty lay and it ate at him inside. Zac shut his eyes, his wife and son's names held on his lips. He stayed for them—to make things right for them.

He offered a slight nod to the waiting director.

"I suppose the better question is, how long have you had them unlocked?"

"A few hours."

"And?"

He continued to stare at the darkness of the Archive, at the black past threatening to engulf him. "Why?"

"You know why."

Zac shook his head and screamed at the man, "I mean, why now? Why all this with the field team and Metcalf? All of it!"

"Time."

"Excuse me?"

Sullivan approached, slow and deliberate. "There comes a point when time stops working with you and starts pushing against your efforts. Eventually, the number of days ahead falls short of the ones behind you. Time is against me, Mr. Modine."

"That's what this is to you? A Holy Grail?"

"For me? No," Sullivan scoffed. "But for the world? We have the opportunity to be remembered as the men that changed history, Zac."

Legacy. It was how the world perceived you, recalled your accomplishments long after your end. That was what it was about. When Zac thought about Sullivan's enduring legacy, there would be plenty to remember. Metcalf and Lincoln. Riley and Morgan. The agents Sullivan had sacrificed to make his dream a reality.

He wanted to run. He wanted to kick and scream, to race for the exits and never look back. Claire and Alex counted on him though. He had already let both of them down enough.

"The Wellspring, Zac," Sullivan pressed. He pointed to the waiting stairwell, the path clear. "Where is it?"

"Stop," Zac said.

"Excuse me?"

"Stop saying *it*." Zac pulled away from the man and started for the stairs. Sullivan followed, looking clearly bemused. The frustrated tech swallowed hard before continuing. "You said it before, but I missed it. 1968 and the microprocessor. Fission in the 30s. Some*one* had to give those to us. Not something. Not an it." From the files unlocked and the documents uncovered from Metcalf's locked directories, Zac knew the truth. "The Wellspring is a *she*. You're saying someone is manipulating our development as a species. Pushing us forward in a specific direction."

"Zac…"

"Yet you didn't trust me enough to tell me."

Sullivan rubbed at his beard. "I had to be sure I could count on you."

"Are you sure now?" Zac yelled. "I believed you and your promises! I believed it all. I betrayed Lincoln…"

"You wear your doubts on your sleeve, Zac," Sullivan replied. A hand guided Zac toward the stairs. "I couldn't take the chance, but now I see my error in that decision. Now where is she?"

The files offered a starting point, but little in the way of actual intel. No, the files were nothing more than a red herring. The truth lay in a text Metcalf had received from an anonymous number around the time the Wellspring had gone missing and again just a few hours ago. The phone was most likely a burner, but the cell tower transmitting the message was clear with a location.

"Maine," he muttered, unable to pick his gaze up from the floor. "A town called Blue Hill."

Sullivan peered up the stairs. The long shadow of a squad of security personnel waited at the top. "You heard the man."

The closest, a tall man with piercing eyes, locked on Zac before nodding to Sullivan. "We're on it."

"You said they were occupied. That they—"

Sullivan stopped Zac from the questions to come. His smile grew. "It's time to go, Zac."

"We can't just leave! What about the others? What about—?"

Sullivan squeezed the man's shoulder, swallowing hard. "We are so close now, Zac. Embrace the path laid before us. You have given it to us. The future waits for no man."

He started through the researcher's hub, analysts peering up from their workstations for only a moment to catch his ego on full display. Zac hesitated. The dead man below called to him. He begged Zac to make things right.

It's all about loyalty now.

Zac had chosen his side. Yet with each step into the light he wondered about the dead and the ultimate cost for Sullivan's perfect future.

CHAPTER TWENTY-EIGHT

Ben's fingers slipped. The push and pull of the air swirled around him. Fingernails dug helplessly into the fourth-floor window ledge of the abandoned school. He fought to gain ground as he reached for the shattered pane for leverage. His feet searched for a ledge. The thin soles of his sneakers scraped against the brick of the building without success. Each movement brought a shooting pain to his side. The lack of pressure on his gaping wound allowed blood to pour down his side like a leaky faucet.

Hendricks stood over him. Even in the darkness his smile and yellowed teeth beamed at his flailing victim.

"You're like a damn cockroach, Riley," Hendricks yelled over the howling wind ripping through the back alley of the school. His foot rose over Ben's outstretched fingers, excitement in his eyes. "But I think if I stomp hard enough I'll hear a squish. What do you think?"

The heel of a boot crunched his right hand. Ben cried out as he slipped from the edge. His left was still in place and the swirling wind helped push him tight to the wall for a moment. He tried to reach for the ledge, but Hendricks' foot kicked away his pitiful attempts. Brown eyes pleaded through the dark. His hand fell limply to his side and refused to come back up. With each second his left struggled to maintain its hold on the brick. Hendricks' enthusiasm grew at the drama unfolding beneath him.

"I can't believe you've lasted this long, Riley," he continued. "After stumbling on the Trust's operations in Buffalo? Yeah, that house on Wex was theirs. It was a moveable resource to hide the Wellspring and other long-term projects. But, man, when you showed up?"

His laughter filled the air. "Sullivan wanted you dead for that one. The guy you chased inside? That was one of his. Sullivan was trying to steal the Wellspring right from his own group. But he screwed up, drew too much attention. The Trust cleaned up the mess without ever realizing it was his to begin with. Lucky bastard. You, though? Not so much. They took everything from you. Well, almost everything. They saved the last bit for me."

Ben swallowed every word, every revelation over his lost life.

"Come on, Riley!" Hendricks exclaimed. Ben cursed under his breath, drawing ire from the mercenary. "Where's the sarcasm now? Where's that belligerent-ass behavior that suits you so well? Give me something!"

Ben called out, but his answer was lost in the wind.

Hendricks shifted closer, his figure looming over the thin ledge. "What?"

"I said 'gladly.'"

"No…" Hendricks' eyes widened. By the time he noticed what Ben's fallen right hand carried, there was nowhere for him to turn—nowhere to avoid what came next. Ben held tight to the gun and pulled the trigger.

The force of the shot almost knocked him clear from the building. Ben held the ledge with two fingers. His blood slowly mixed with the mortar between each brick.

The bullet had found its mark, catching the dumbfounded Hendricks between the eyes. His body staggered on the edge of the window frame, and he looked unsure how to process what happened. Then the forward lean of the all-too-eager mercenary forced his body into the waiting air. The frozen stare of the man who had inflicted so much pain on Ben over the last few hours floated past him, into the night sky, and down to the parking lot below. Refusing to follow him, Ben dropped the gun and grabbed hold of the ledge once more. The wind threatened to send him after his assailant. When he heard the crash of the lifeless body of Connor Hendricks against the pavement, he allowed himself a slight smile.

Every movement was agony. Every inch he climbed drove daggers through his body. His screams filled the air, drowning out all other sound. Ben pulled with every ounce of strength left. He fought through the blood and sweat, inching his tired and broken form toward the shattered fourth-floor window of the abandoned school. Shards of glass dug into his skin, yet he refused to pause. He dragged his body deeper into the building with each forced breath.

The weightlessness faded with the arrival of solid ground. Ben took a moment to glance back outside, to capture the image of Hendricks down below. His lifeless body was sprawled upon the concrete, face up to the heavens with wide eyes pleading for help that would never arrive.

"Christ, Hendricks. Didn't your mother ever teach you to shut your mouth?"

He tried to find his feet and shuffled into the vacant classroom proper. Two steps in, he collapsed, his legs no longer supporting anything. Ben's hand dropped from his side. Stains of blood ran along his shirt and down his torn pant leg. He fell to the floor with a loud thud. Darkness filled his vision. Deep shadows danced before him.

Then he laughed. A thick, blood-spewed bout of joy exited his swollen lips. *How's that for belligerent-ass behavior, Hendricks?*

The smile remained, thick and dark from the blood caked to his teeth. Ben's eyes, however, closed to the world.

CHAPTER TWENTY-NINE

Sullivan and Zac vacated the building, the full force of the Security Division ahead of them. It was only in the silence of their departure that the Witness stepped out of the shadows. The secret hatch in the wall closed and he carefully crept along the wall to stay out of sight. Personnel occupied the researcher's hub. From his position he could hear the murmurs of gossip passing between employees as to the current state of the department.

The Witness pitied them; their small lives were oblivious to what occurred around them. Sullivan's power play had put them in jeopardy, though the fault truly lay with the Witness now. He had let this happen by not moving quickly enough and not being thorough enough in his planning. It was time to start fixing his mistake.

He set off the fire alarm. The clanging of multiple bells filled the floor in seconds. Strobe lighting from the alarms ran from every corner. The bells were joined by the pattering of heels against the tile.

Dozens rushed for the exit, eyes locked on the outside world. He filtered between them. None questioned why someone would be driving deeper into the building when the alarms howled for them to flee. They simply ran out and left their work, their purpose, and their great tasks for their own safety. They never looked back, and never considering the possibility of a false alarm.

The Witness stood alone in the hub. Dozens of terminals surrounded him—all fed through a central operations platform. All were utterly useless. It was technology used to solve and aid sister agencies around the country while maintaining the DSA's secrecy. The technology turned out to be nothing more than a wall, obstructing the DSA's view of the outside world until it was too late. All this technology had replaced the free spirit behind the organization's inception: the unanswered questions sought after by a select few. Now technology led to nothing but compromise and secrets. The DSA had paid the price for both.

No longer.

It was time to change things. The Witness headed for the lower level of the facility. He rounded the corridor, stopping at the end of the loop in front of the open door to the Archive.

And the dead man within.

The Witness removed his thick glasses, then rubbed at the scar tissue adorning his eyes. Lincoln was dead and it was the Witness' fault.

He had hoped for a different outcome. Even after all these years he held out for hope — what he saw as the ultimate flaw in humanity. He had hoped Lincoln would not hesitate when he confronted Sullivan. He had tried to warn him not to question the mission, not to doubt himself, but the Witness had failed. All Lincoln had to do was pull the trigger. It would have ended so much: not only Sullivan's life but the search for the Wellspring. The coup of the DSA would have been over hours after it had begun. If only Lincoln had listened to the Witness. If only he had truly believed in his warnings about the future.

Instead, history repeated itself, despite the Witness' efforts.

Lincoln was dead and there was no changing it. Instead, the Witness made the best of the situation. He lowered the duffel bag he had collected from the men's room upon his arrival. Unzipping the main compartment, he then reached inside and removed the first of six spherical charges.

When he had jostled the items on their staging area earlier that day it wasn't by accident. He had deliberately played into Lincoln's paranoia enough to get him to slip the devices into his bag. There were no accidents in the universe — none that escaped the Witness' savvy glare, at any rate. There was only the truth and the path ahead.

The charges were necessary, though Lincoln had never realized why. A precaution, an overzealous desire to anticipate any outcome, had forced the agent to pack the explosives along with so many other trinkets. It was exactly as the Witness had intended.

"Thank you for trying, Lincoln. You are a better man than I gave you credit for," the Witness whispered in the dark. He bent down, the first charge in his hand. He placed the device on Lincoln's chest and set the timer. "Your sacrifice will not be forgotten."

He hated it: the feeling of blood on his hands. It would always be there, though; it would always be necessary in order for the work to continue. Lincoln's sacrifice had opened the door to a new option. The alarms and the explosives would see to that.

What came next would be up to him.

Shuffling through the lower level of the complex, the Witness placed the charges along the structural beams central to the DSA warehouse. The timers beeped under the blaring alarms as the lone figure made one last lap of the lower level.

The plaques stopped him. Names stretched before his eyes. Dates were listed beneath, but none of the details of their demise were mentioned. More sacrifices. All in the search for a greater truth. Fingers grazed the frames, trailing them back through history from the most recent until settling along the oldest. The date read 1973. The name was barely a memory.

His name.

He pulled the plaque away and tucked it in the bag at his side. Then he rushed up the stairs, through the hub, and toward the front entrance. Sirens rang in the distance. More lights from emergency vehicles rounded nearby corners for the premises. The Witness reached the crowd gathered in the parking lot and filtered between them.

Positioned among them, the enigmatic figure faced the building once more. He had never lied to Lincoln. With the Wellspring in hand and the power of the DSA's information at his disposal, Sullivan stood poised to change history, and not for the better.

The Witness checked his watch.

The equation just changed.

The sound of the explosives caused the crowd to silence, reeling back and away from the building. The low bursts grew, rumbling higher along the support structure of the inner walls. The explosions continued, rising—dirt and debris showered the parking lot surrounding the empty warehouse.

Then the building collapsed. In and away from the mass of spectators, the DSA crumbled. The sound echoed for blocks; the dust cloud rose and was observed for miles all around. The Department of Special Assignments had hidden in plain sight for over ten years under the authority of Susan Metcalf. It had failed to last a single day under Greg Sullivan.

The DSA was dead, and the Witness smiled.

"Long live the DSA."

He faded into the confusion, his next plan already forming.

CHAPTER THIRTY

She arrived in time to witness the fall. The exterior monitors of the warehouse displayed the carnage. Concrete walls collapsed, and dust and debris rose up in thick clouds. Panicked faces rushed for the far side of the parking lot, looking to escape the destruction.

The shovel clanged at her side. The wet and dirty instrument echoed in the solitude of the bunker. Metcalf stumbled away from it, grime and tears covering her face. When she had left the warehouse the last time, hope had rested in her eyes. She had hoped to rectify her mistakes and see a way back to the work. She had always envisioned a light at the end of the tunnel no matter how far in the distance it might have seemed. Now, the path ahead appeared forever darkened. Everything had fallen apart—from loyalties to the mortar holding her department together.

Sullivan had taken it all.

The metal stairs clattered beneath her boots. Then, she slipped. Her right knee, still troubled from the car wreck that had served as her escape from Sullivan's grasp, locked up and she missed the next step. She crashed to the ground.

Cold tile soothed her cheek as she lay in bitter defeat. The sound of the collapsing structure continued to ring throughout the chamber and echo in her mind. Unmoving, succumbing to the events of the singular day, Metcalf sobbed.

She cried for Jacob Grissom. Her bullet had ended his life as much as her orders from months earlier. She had loved him, depended on him for so long, yet she had been forced to watch him fall as so many others had during her tenure. Just like Stephanie

Atwater. The woman's blood still coated Metcalf's fingers, still soaked her jacket; it was a constant reminder of her failure. She had always asked more of others than she could ever bring to the table. She had always demanded the truth when she offered nothing more than lies.

It was all for the illusion of control.

She believed in their mission. In finding the Wellspring, and discovering the truth behind her purpose. That was another failure. It was another opportunity lost in the collapse of everything she had built over the last decade. The DSA had been nothing before her; it had only been a contingent of obsessive agents of disparate organizations working on their own time to uncover secrets no one else imagined possible. It had been a reckless, antiquated model she had reconfigured to bring the department the legitimacy it deserved. To play a larger role in the conflict to come.

Now it was gone. Like ash in the wind, the warehouse — her true home — was no more.

Metcalf slammed her fist against the floor. A scream ripped from her lips, demanding satisfaction. She struggled to her knees, grasping at loose furniture for support. Her legs wanted to collapse under the weight, under the unbearable pain of the sacrifices that had been required to feed her ego. She refused to heed any of them — refused to wallow in misery.

Grissom and Atwater. Lincoln and Ruth. Even Morgan and Ben. So many had been lost along the way. Who would be next? How could she ask anyone to follow her further? How could she expect anyone else to make the next sacrifice for the so-called greater good? What did it even matter anymore?

Fires burned on the monitors. Emergency vehicles approached the wreckage in the distance to put out the blaze she had set long ago through her ignorance. The DSA was a failure. Hers and hers alone.

A chirping sound snapped her from her solemn thoughts. On the briefing table, Metcalf's phone vibrated with the arrival of a new voicemail. She wiped away the tears and the exhaustion from the day, then lifted the device. A text message previously missed sat on the screen and she scanned the words quickly.

She's stopped.

Eyes widened. She pounded at the keyboard. *Where?*

Blue Hill, Maine.

"It's time," she said to the emptiness of the bunker. "After so long, it's time."

She understood the text message immediately. The Wellspring, after days of constant movement, had come to rest. For Metcalf, it was the culmination of a decade of searching. All thought of failure faded. The sorrow threatening to drown her drained away and was replaced by something new. This was no longer the time for self-recrimination. This was the time to act—to right the mistakes of the past. That was the purpose of the bunker, of the entire protocol established with Stephanie.

A second chance.

The same she offered to everyone recruited to the department. It was time to earn hers.

How?

The monitors continued to display the destruction, but they no longer held her attention. She scanned the floor, peering around each corner. Duffel bags were set along the railing. Supplies and equipment had been positioned all around in preparation for this day. All had been put together by a dead woman—the very last sacrifice, if Metcalf had anything to say about it.

She would not let Stephanie's death be marred by failure, to see her sacrifice be in vain. It was time to change. It was time to trust in others to stand with her.

Morgan was right.

Morgan Dunleavy, who held no fear over the agencies hunting her. Her only concern was focused on the man left behind. The man willing to stand alone to save them all.

Metcalf started for the exit, pain in every staggered step. She couldn't leave Morgan behind. Not with the Wellspring so close, not with answers finally in reach after so long.

"I'm coming, Morgan," Metcalf whispered in the solitude of the bunker. She had to help, to take a stand, and make things right.

She only hoped she wasn't too late.

CHAPTER THIRTY-ONE

The ride back to Bethesda was a blur. There were constant shadows on the periphery. Morgan imagined enemies all around her, but she didn't care—couldn't care. Not with Ben in danger. She put everything else on hold. Zac's betrayal, Stephanie's death, and Grissom's confession screamed for acknowledgment, but she ignored them all.

Ben needed her. That was all that mattered.

The fall of a stark, black figure against the glowing moon above grabbed her attention. The fall caused her to slam on the brakes outside the chain-link fence of the school. The body arced in the sky, suspended in the air for a long moment before it dropped to the ground with a dull crash. The man was dead before impact; she could tell by the way his hands failed to protect his body during the descent. There was also the lack of a blood-curdling scream. The event was out of her control, though she rushed to his side nonetheless.

She recognized him immediately. A surprised look was frozen on Connor Hendricks' face, his eyes wide. He stared into the night sky, pleading with some unseen force.

Where Grissom had come for her as the ghost of her past, it seemed Ben had faced his personal demon in the form of Hendricks. He appeared to have handled things on his own. Following Hendricks' lost glance to the heavens, Morgan found her partner dangling from the ledge of the fourth floor. He struggled to pull himself up. His weary body fought against his efforts.

"Ben!" she called before rushing into the building.

Her flashlight guided her up the stairwell, and she gripped her Glock tight in her other hand. She took the stairs two at a time until she made it to the top floor of the school. Sneakers squealed against dirty tiles as she headed toward the only open door at the end of the corridor.

When she reached the classroom, she took the turn too sharply. Her arm slammed against the frame of the door. A curse escaped her lips, and the flashlight slid from her hand. It rolled along the empty expanse of the room until it came to rest near the shattered window, illuminating the figure on the floor.

"Ben!" His chest barely rose. A smile on his face fought to shine through. It was as if he was laughing at his own joke—just like always. Morgan was at his side in an instant. "No, no, no…"

Morgan ripped open his shirt, the fabric soaked in blood. She found two entry wounds. One was a through and through along his bicep. Not a deal breaker. But the one on his side? That was another story. His breathing was shallow.

"Don't you even think about it, you ass," Morgan said. Her left hand collapsed against the bullet wound on his side. Her right went for his carotid to check his vitals.

His chest stopped rising.

"Ben!" Her screams echoed down the hall. Her hands pumped in syncopated rhythm on his chest.

"Stay with me, dammit," Morgan muttered between compressions. His eyes refused to open. His lungs refused to breathe. Still she fought through the darkness around them, unwilling to surrender after everything they had fought through together.

Stay with me.

ABOUT THE AUTHOR

Lou Paduano is the author of the Greystone series of urban fantasy adventures, which follow Detective Greg Loren and Soriya Greystone as they hunt myths, monsters, and legends in the city of Portents.

He is also the author of the conspiracy thriller series, The DSA, a serialized tale about a clandestine government agency trying to discover the true power behind humanity's future.

He lives in Grand Island, New York with his wife and three daughters. Sign up for his e-mail list for free content as well as updates on future releases at loupaduano.com.

THE GREYSTONE SAGA

AVAILABLE NOW

Follow the adventures of Soriya Greystone and Detective Greg Loren as they hunt dangerous myths and legends in the city of Portents.

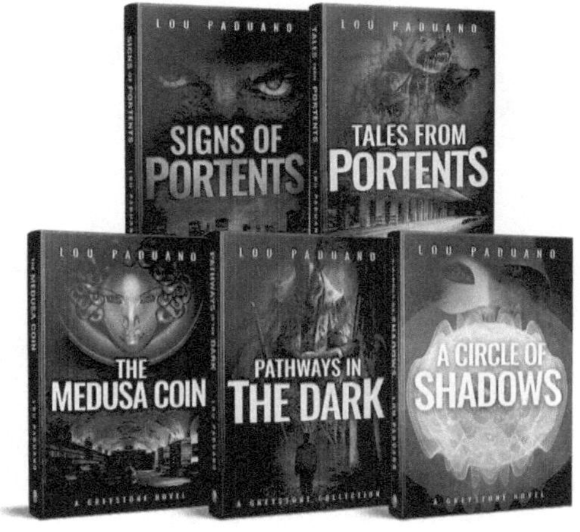

BOOK ONE - SIGNS OF PORTENTS
BOOK TWO - TALES FROM PORTENTS
BOOK THREE - THE MEDUSA COIN
BOOK FOUR - PATHWAYS IN THE DARK
BOOK FIVE - A CIRCLE OF SHADOWS

THE DSA CONTINUES IN…

Ben Riley lies near death.

Having done all she can to save her partner's life, Morgan Dunleavy is faced with an even greater emergency: the Wellspring has been captured by Greg Sullivan.

In a desperate gambit to free the enigmatic figure, who may be the key component behind humanity's scientific and technological advancement over the centuries, Morgan must infiltrate the enemy stronghold alone.

Even if she succeeds in saving the mysterious woman, Morgan still faces the treason charges leveled against not only herself, but the entire DSA.

Susan Metcalf, however, has a plan to save them all that will change the DSA forever.

www.ingramcontent.com/pod-product-compliance
Lightning Source LLC
Chambersburg PA
CBHW032032180726
48284CB00008B/2557